Blind date

By Katharine E. Hamilton

ISBN-13: 978-1-7358125-5-7

Blind Date

www.katharinehamilton.com

Cover Design by Kerry Prater.

This is a work of fiction. Names, characters, places, and incidents are either the product of the author's imagination or are used factiously, and any resemblance to actual persons, living or dead, business establishments, events or locales is entirely coincidental.

For my friends.
You know who you are.

I met my husband in 2006. I didn't know he would end up being my husband. In fact, I didn't know I'd even want to date him when I first met him. That sort of all evolved over time. What *did* happen, was a good friend urged me to join her for a fun night at a cool bar with some cool people.

I met my husband that night, sitting around a small fire pit, trying to keep warm, and unknowingly melting the soles off my favorite boots.

It would be years later when we'd actually admit to our feelings for one another. It would take even more years after that before we took the plunge and married. But I would have never met him if my friend had not invited, convinced, dragged me to a party one Saturday night.

Sometimes our friends know
what we need before we do.

Acknowledgments

Thank you to everyone who shared their dating/blind date/courting ups and downs for the funny stories, the sweet stories, and the absolutely horrific.

Thank you to my cover designer, Kerry Prater. I texted her, "Hey, I have this book... I want it done this week." And she delivered.

Thank you to my editor, Lauren Hanson.

Thank you to my beta readers! They're always up for another one of my books, even ones that never see the light of day. Thanks, ladies!

Date #1

"So, really, hedge funds are the way to go if you're serious about making real money." His voice droned on about the risk and excitement of working with the money of other people and how "stellar" he was at his job. Evangelina Harper bit back a groan as she twirled her fork in her remaining pasta. It was her third time to have pasta for the week, and if she hadn't already lost her appetite listening to her date chomp on his crunchy crab legs, she would have lost it by simply plucking the loose tendril of hair from her overly cooked noodles. The place wasn't a dive, but it also wasn't a place Lina would have chosen if she'd been given the opportunity. But, with blind dates, she rarely had the privilege of choosing the location. She'd recently dined at various restaurants all across the city, from the finest and fanciest to the ones that made her stomach turn when she stepped inside. This one fell somewhere towards the latter. And her date, Mr. Hedge Fund Extraordinaire, seemed more in love with himself than interested in a date. Or money... he seemed rather attracted to money, and how much Lina made, more than anything else about her. She wasn't quite interested in the beady-eyed man across from her. He seemed ambitious, which isn't always a bad thing, but ambition mixed with greed flirted with disastrous, and she wasn't interested in a disaster. But she'd promised Andy she'd give it a go. Ten blind dates. That's what she'd committed to, with full reports from all of them so Andy would be convinced Lina had indeed given dating a chance.

Not that she minded dating. She didn't, it just wasn't her priority. But her best friend and roommate, Andy, had recently found love and now felt determined that everyone else in her life needed to as well. Top of her list: Lina. And so here Lina sat, now learning the ins and outs of insider trading. She glanced at her watch and felt a flood of relief to see that she'd stuck the date out for over an hour. She reached for her glass and took a sip before reaching for her handbag. The man straightened, his eyes curious, as he watched her rest her napkin on the table to stand. "I'm so sorry to have to cut this short," Lina apologized. "It's an early day for me tomorrow. It was a pleasure to meet you, Dean."

"It's Dan," he corrected, those pointed eyes studying her as thouugh she were a rare specimen of weird.

"Right. Dan." She tapped her temple. "It was nice meeting you." She slipped her jacket on and tucked her handbag in the inside pocket. "Take care." She noticed him starting to stand and rushed her last little wave, so as to avoid any further small talk or the dreaded "after date hug" that seemed to follow all dates... even the bad ones.

"I didn't even get—" she heard him call after her, but she didn't stop and hurried out the door and out onto the sidewalk, breathing in the fresh, cold air. She looked up and embraced the escape for mere seconds before she felt her phone buzz in her purse. She knew it was Andy. Clearly *Dan* had already called to express his disappointment in her abrupt departure. The call could wait. Stuffing her hands in her jacket pockets, Lina scurried her way towards the metro, disappeared down the steps and into the tunnels, and headed towards home. One blind date down, nine more to go.

Date #2

"I think it's so fascinating that you work at a publishing house. It must be so interesting to read all the books before they're published."

"Sometimes." Lina glanced up as the waiter placed their glasses on the table and hurried off again.

"I admit, I was a bit nervous in meeting you tonight."

"Really? Why is that?"

"Well, I didn't want you to think I agreed to this date based on what you do for a living."

"And why would I have thought that?"

"Because I'm a writer." He beamed proudly across the table. His smile, a nice one, Lina noted, was charming, in a teenage-heartthrob kind of way. She pictured him being the cute guy in high school and college, the one who'd surprised everyone by ditching the baseball scholarship and going for a liberal arts degree. She could be wrong, but from what she just heard, she doubted it.

"A writer?"

"Yep."

"And are you published?" she asked.

"Well, not yet," he admitted. "But I plan to be. I've been working on this space opera fantasy that just—"

And there it was, Lina thought with disappointment. *The pitch*. The moment. That small slash in the evening that told her the date wasn't going to work. This guy, to his credit, lasted twenty-two minutes before being mentally cut from her mind. Unfortunately, she hadn't even finished her meal yet. But the good thing about fantasy writers, she mused, was that they could never sum up their work in progress in just a few short sentences. She was in for a long explanation, and as he discussed the eleven kingdoms of dwarves, elves, and aliens, and the expanse of his universe, she knew she had plenty of time to indulge in the perfectly smoked salmon gracing her plate.

She'd give him points for choosing an awesome location. The seafood joint was comfortable, casual, and had remarkable food. So she'd listen to his story, literally, and give him the typical industry encouragement and then cross him off Andy's list of potentials. She went through her mental to-do list, realizing she'd forgotten to grant her assistant's time off request. She made a mental note to do that the next morning. She also realized what was missing in the current manuscript she'd been working on. She'd been asked to provide a developmental edit of the piece, and there was one passage in particular that needed work and had her stumped for days. It clicked, then, what she needed to do to flesh it out more. She added that to the list. Tuning back into the conversation, she heard the intricacies of the spacecraft that housed the hero of his story. The detail was there, but too much so. Fantasy wasn't her favorite genre. She mostly worked on historical fiction projects at work, though every now and then a lovely romance or women's literature passed over her desk, but fantasy was an entirely different ball game. Mostly because the editing phase of those projects took forever due to *all* the excessive detail into the smallest things. The knobs in the cockpit, the face shields on the spacesuits... every detail carved out, even when not necessary.

Two hours later, Lina found herself walking into her apartment, exhausted, annoyed, and grumbling, when she spotted Andy watching a fantasy television show. She'd had enough fantasy for one night. Another date down, only eight more to go.

Date #3

"Do you work out? You look like you work out."

Lina choked on her sip of water, before dabbing a napkin over her lips. "I'm sorry?"

"Andy said you really like running. I love to run. I've participated in the marathon the last three years. Do you run marathons?"

"No, actually, I don't. I don't enjoy running."

"But Andy said you run all the time."

"I do, but that doesn't mean I enjoy it." Lina chuckled at his baffled expression. "I'm sorry, I know that sounds weird."

"A little." He smiled, his eyes bouncing from one feature to the next as he studied her face. She squirmed under the survey. "What about working out? You didn't say. Do you enjoy that? It's important to me that whomever I get involved with enjoys fitness to some degree. Because, well, it's my life and career."

"I understand that." Lina perked up at that. "It's how I am with books. The book world is my life and work and I've always wanted to be with someone who enjoys reading and discussing books."

His facial expression told her he was not that guy.

"Do fitness magazines count?"

She grimaced, though kept the conversation light. "Not really."

"I'm not much of a reader," he admitted. "In fact, I can't tell you how long it's been since I've read an actual book. Probably because it's a stagnant and lazy hobby."

"Excuse me?" Her spine snapped straight in her chair.

"Think about it, you just sit there holding a book. That does nothing for your heart rate."

"I disagree. You're using your mind."

He scoffed. "Are you about to give me the 'your brain is the largest muscle' speech?"

"No. I wasn't. There are audiobooks for people who have a more active lifestyle or even for those who do not like sitting and reading a book or a tablet. You could be running and listening to a book at the same time."

His brow raised. "Good point. I'll give you that one." He smirked. "But it would have to be ground-breaking to get me back into even listening to a book."

"That's a shame." Lina smoothed a hand over her lap as she remembered she'd forgotten to pick up her dry cleaning on the way home from work earlier in the day. It was too late now to pick it up, but it wasn't too late to stop for an ice cream on the way back to her apartment. Alone.

The waiter slid the bill onto the table in a suave and smooth gesture on his way towards his other customers. Lina's relief must have shown.

"I guess we can both agree that this is just a one night gig, huh?" the man asked.

"I think you're right."

"Well, at least you're honest." He grinned, plopping some cash on the table for the ticket. "So, my place or yours?"

Appalled at his assumption, Lina stood and gathered her purse with disgust etched on her face, ending date number three before he could think of other activities for them to partake in together. Three blind dates down, seven more to go.

Date #4

"A spare. Not bad." Rick grinned at her as he slipped his fingers into the holes of his own bowling ball and stepped to the lane for his turn.

Lina watched as he expertly flicked his wrist and sent the ball careening down the glossy wooden lane and straight into the leading pin. A clear strike that demolished all the pins in one swoop. He turned with a cheeky smile and she clapped.

"Bravo. You're better at this than you let on." She stood, walking towards the ball return and waited for her pink ball to emerge.

"I come here a lot with friends," he admitted. "It's laidback fun that helps me escape from work every once in a while."

"Stocks, was it?" Lina asked.

"Floor trader, yes."

"I bet that is intense." She retrieved her ball and walked to the lane, lining up her body with the pins. She then took two steps, brought her arm back, and released her roll. She watched as her ball veered to the left and knocked out the farthest two pins. She waited again at the ball return. Rick watched her closely, but she didn't mind. She could tell he was assessing her throw and not her figure, which made the moment less awkward.

"You're crossing your arm too far in front of you. That's why it keeps going that way."

"I noticed that too. I don't know why I do that." She smiled as she tapped her foot in anticipation of her ball coming to her. So far, she'd had a fun evening with Rick. They didn't have the typical dinner date. Instead, cheesy nachos loaded down with jalapenos and shredded chicken at the bowling alley was their feast. And it was delicious. He was kind, good looking in the smart, tailored business-suit guy kind of way. Though he wore jeans and a polo now, she could tell the clothes were not his normal wardrobe. He held himself tall and straight, his hair perfectly in place, and his hands somewhat soft from just holding a pen most days. But even that didn't bother her about him. Dare she say she actually liked Rick? It had been over an hour and she'd yet to look for an escape, which was a promising sign. Maybe Andy got this one right. Lina's ball spit through the return and she walked to the lane, concentrating on her posture and position of her arm. Rick stepped up beside her.

"May I?" he asked, pointing towards her arm.

She nodded and he stepped to the side of her, his arm curved around her body, and his hand resting on top of her wrist that held the ball. She wished she felt something at his touch, a tingle, or goose flesh, or something, but she didn't. A classic date move on his part, but she wasn't put off by it. She just didn't feel anything. Disappointed, but not discouraged, she allowed him to guide her toss, the ball moving slower but straight towards the pins. It found the center pin and slowly one pin after another began to fall until all were down. "A spare!" she cheered. "I'm at least getting good at those." She raised her hand to give him a high five, only he tugged her hand and pulled her towards him, planting a firm kiss on her lips in celebration. She froze as warning bells rang in her head. And as he pulled away from her, his eyes danced. She forced a smile and took a couple of steps back as he reached for his own ball and began lining up his throw.

She was not a "kiss on the first date" kind of girl. Nor was she a "kiss a stranger" kind of girl. He hadn't even asked her. Which, she guessed was kind of silly to presume he would. And the date had been going well... but to just *kiss* her over a throw? Seemed a bit premature. And a bit hasty in her book. Andy would scold her, she knew, but Rick just axed himself off the list. Four dates down, six more to go.

Date #5

Lina jumped to her feet and cheered with the crowd as the New York Knicks scored a three-point shot to end the second quarter sending them into half time with the lead against the Boston Celtics. Though she inwardly liked the Celtics better, her ticket had been for the Knicks, so she sported a jersey and chanted the cheers. Her inward betrayal to Larry Byrd would just have to be sorted out later. She loved basketball, but she rarely treated herself to a game. Caleb, the man beside her yelling in glee was a season ticket holder, according to Andy, so it was no surprise Lina found herself at a game. He smiled in her direction as they found their seats. "Crazy shot, right?"

"Impressive is more like it," she replied.

"Hey, thanks for coming with me tonight. I know it's not exactly dinner and a movie."

"Are you kidding? I much prefer this."

He liked her answer because he turned in his seat to face her more directly.

"I love basketball," Lina continued. "I played when I was younger but have always loved watching it."

"And how are you still single?" Caleb asked.

She laughed, waving away his comment.

"No, really," he continued. "You're beautiful, successful, kind, you love sports…" He started tallying her traits on his fingers. "Where've you been hiding, Evangelina Harper?"

"In an office on the twenty-third floor."

He smirked at her reply and she liked the way his blue eyes danced over her face. Restaurants, Lina reminded herself. According to Andy, Caleb owned several chain taco restaurants throughout New York City. Which surprised Lina further that she didn't find herself sitting inside one of those, but instead, having a blast at a basketball game. Points to him for not rubbing his profession in her face. The buzzer sounded, signaling the end of half time and the third quarter commenced. The lead bounced back and forth between the two teams, which made for an exciting game and fun interactions with fellow Knicks fans as each goal sank through the net.

When the remaining few seconds of the game ticked by, and the Knicks were one shot away from tying or winning the game, Lina felt Caleb's hand clench hers in nervous anticipation as they watched the Knicks pass the ball up the court to an open man. Defensive Celtics attempted an interception and missed, leaving Knicks fans at the edge of their seats as their star player went up for a jumping three-point shot for the win. The ball soared through the air, all fans holding a collective breath, as they watched it tap the rim of the basket and bounce around before falling to the floor and not sinking through the net for a shot. The buzzer sounded. The Knicks had lost.

"You've got to be kidding me!" Caleb shouted. He released Lina's hand to pull at the sides of his hair as he began to rant, curse, stomp, and spit in the direction of the Knicks bench several rows in front of them. He wasn't the only one. He, along with several other angry fans, raged. Horrified, Lina watched his public tantrum. He wasn't the only disgruntled fan, but his once pretty blue eyes seethed like a mad man. She ducked out of the row and mixed into the exiting crowd as she wound her way through the arena and to her escape. She mentally scratched his name off the list, reaffirmed her love for Larry Byrd, and left. Five dates down, five to go.

Date #6

"Cheers." Brett toasted his glass to hers and they took a sip of wine as the instructor set up her canvas and began showing the class which picture they'd be painting for the night. Creative date, check. Handsome date, check. Seemed nice, check.

Lina went through the list of points in Brett's favor as she focused on the paint colors being squirted into her tray by the instructor's assistant. She'd heard of these painting while sipping wine events, and she thought it sounded like fun. Now she'd finally know. Though she didn't know much about art, or have much art of her own, the idea of creating something on a blank canvas intrigued her.

"So, are you secretly an artist?" Lina asked.

Brett laughed. "Not quite. A friend told me about this place, and it sounded like something different."

Lina watched the instructor paint a yellow arch across her canvas and attempted the same technique on her own. "It is different. I like the idea."

"I'm glad." He grinned at her.

"So how do you know Andy?" Lina asked.

"College. We took a few classes together."

"That was a long time ago. You guys stayed in touch?"

"Well, I'm new to the city. I saw on social media that she lived here and reached out a while back for tips, suggestions, and help with finding a place to live. She was helpful, and it was fun to reconnect."

"So how long have you been here?"

"About six months now."

"And do you like it?" Lina asked.

"I love it. Definitely my speed."

They switched brushes and began applying a light orange to their picture, the giant sun beginning to take shape.

"So where do you plan on hanging your masterpiece?" Lina asked.

"Over my mantle, of course."

"You have a fireplace? In New York City?"

He laughed. "No. I have a furnace that barely works half the time. But I like to pretend I can afford a place with a fireplace."

She chuckled. "Don't we all."

"Now take your smaller brush and dip it into the black paint." The instructor began making long strokes in the corner of her canvas. "A beautiful tree emerges as you make the strokes. Be adventurous with your strokes. Branches don't have to make sense."

"This is going to be an interesting image."

"That it will be." Lina leaned back to survey her work. "I might give it to Andy."

He laughed as he glanced at her terrible tree picture. "Totally do that."

She nudged his shoulder as he stifled his laugh.

After another half hour, the instructor placed her brush down and clapped her hands. "Twenty-minute break for the paint to dry a bit before we begin working on the foreground. Please, help yourself to refreshments."

Lina sighed as she placed her brush in the water cup at her station. She turned to talk with Brett and spotted him already out of his seat and across the room chatting with an attractive blonde by the wine cart. He topped off the woman's glass and proceeded to flash his charming smile until the woman handed him a small white piece of paper containing her phone number. Brett pocketed the slip with a pleased smile. Lina's interest immediately deflated. How could he be picking up other women when he was out with her? Yes, they weren't dating exclusively, but he was here *with* her. He walked back over and sat. "Oh, did you need a refill?"

He looked up at her as she stood. "No. I think I'm good." She forced a polite smile as she slipped her jacket off the back of her chair. "I'm just going to get some air right quick."

"Sure thing." He beamed up at her and did not even offer to walk with her.

When Lina stepped outside, she walked to the curb and held out a hand until a cab pulled up beside her. She recited her address to the driver and sank back against the seat. Maybe it was too soon to just leave the date entirely, but Lina was done. If he couldn't even focus on one woman at a time, what was the point? She deserved better. She mentally scratched Brett's name off Andy's list. Six dates down, four more to go.

Chapter One

"Andy, I have already told you no." Evangelina laughed into her cell phone as she waited with fellow pedestrians to cross the busy street. She turned her head from the left to the right to watch as traffic began to slow down as the stoplight changed from green to yellow and then to red. The crosswalk sign flipped to the white dotted outline of a walking man and she began crossing the street at as quick a pace as she could muster in her four-inch heels. She caught a glimpse of her reflection in one of the storefront windows on the sidewalk as she turned to walk towards her work building at the end of the block. She ran a hand through her auburn hair and turned her attention back to her best friend's voice. "Seriously, Andy, how many failed attempts does it take?"

"You promised me ten," Andy replied. "Ten dates. You've only been on six. Mr. Right is out there, Lina. I know he is."

"Remind me again why I'm doing this?"

"Because you love me," Andy teased. "And because I have found love and believe it to be possible. I believe in rainbows and unicorns and butterflies now, remember, so I want the same for you."

Lina rolled her eyes on a snicker. "Right. I forgot about the new Mr. Dreamboat in your life. You've been dating him how long again? If his presence is going to make you want to beat me over the head with testosterone every chance you get, I may not like him."

"You will, I promise. And you will meet him this weekend."

"I better. He's kept you out all hours of the day and night. Stolen our lunch dates, which are our designated time together."

"Um, we live together," Andy reminded her.

"Yeah, our designated time together outside of the house and to support one another amidst our crazy work days."

"Right. True."

"All teasing aside, I'm happy for you," Lina continued. "I just wish your happiness didn't involve finding me happiness."

"Oh, but you love it. How many free meals have you gotten over the last few weeks because of it?"

"I can buy my own meals."

"Okay, well then, how many fun activities have you gotten to do?"

"A few, I guess," Lina admitted, though the thought of attending another blind date made her want to scratch her eyeballs out.

"Listen, we're close. He's just around the corner, I bet."

"It's okay if he's not," Lina countered. "I like being single."

"Said every lonely person in America."

"Not true."

"Okay, maybe not." Andy giggled into the receiver. "But just because you like being single, that doesn't mean you wouldn't like having someone special either."

"We'll see." Evangelina rounded the corner and walked towards her favorite coffee shop. "Listen, I'm grabbing coffee. I'll check with you later."

"Fine. Tell Trevor I said hello. Don't forget tonight. Seven at Mode."

"Joy." Lina's voice dripped sarcasm as she shuffled forward in line awaiting her turn.

"You better show."

"Have I not shown up for any of the others?"

"No. But you did sneak out early on the last one, leaving Brett completely confused."

"Well, maybe he can console himself in the arms of the blonde bombshell. The one whose number he received in the middle of our date."

"Ay yi yi..." Andy sighed. "Okay, fair shot," she chuckled. "Just... don't be late." She hung up before Lina could respond. Lina stuffed her phone into her purse and scanned the menu as she waited her turn in line at the coffee shop. She knew what she wanted, yet she always tried to convince herself to try something new.

"What will it be, Lina?" Trevor, the barista, cast her a flirtatious grin and leaned over the countertop to lightly tug on a piece of her hair that framed her face. She waved his hand away and smiled. "Hey, Trevor. I really want to try something new."

"FINALLY!" He raised his hands in the air as if he were celebrating a long-awaited victory.

She laughed and rolled her eyes. "But I don't know what I want to get, so why don't you surprise me."

"I think I could do that." He quickly went about grabbing ingredients for a caffeinated concoction. "So, Andy came by this morning. Said she was sending you on another blind date tonight." Trevor winked at her as he filled the cup with foaming whipped cream and sprinkled it with cinnamon.

"Don't remind me," Lina grumbled.

"How many is that now?"

"This will be number seven."

"Seven?! You've already had *six*?"

"Yes, and yet she still believes she can find my Mr. Right."

"Well perhaps she might. Who knows, it could be me tonight?" His eyebrows danced as he slid her the cup of joe with an extra shot of espresso over the smooth dark counter.

"I could only hope, Trevor," Lina jested as she stepped out of the way for the next customer to order and to gather a few napkins for the remainder of her walk. In fact, she'd contemplated Trevor before. He was ridiculously good looking, had a fun personality, and he flirted with her every day. Granted, he flirted with pretty much all his female customers, so she couldn't really count herself special, but he was delightful, and she wouldn't count him as a negative option if he did happen to be one of her dates in the future.

∞

He had time. At least that's what he told himself as he followed the pretty brunette up the sidewalk and towards the coffee shop on the corner. He worked up the street. It wasn't a far walk. And if the line wasn't too long, then he could grab a hot coffee and make it to work in plenty of time.

Nathan Alexander listened and watched the beautiful woman in front of him as he made his way across the street, her voice light and humored by her conversation and her steps confident. He had seen her in the mornings before; every morning actually, for the last three weeks. She had never noticed him, or anyone for that matter. If she was not on the phone, she was reading an email on her phone or sorting through stacks of papers as she walked. Not that he was complaining. She was lovely to look at regardless.

Her slim frame all wrapped up in an expensive and fitted business skirt and jacket, taut calves that flexed when she walked in her stiletto heels, the woman was bewitching. He stepped through the open door to the smells of coffee grounds and cinnamon buns and spotted her standing to the side, pulling a few napkins from the holder.

"What can I get ya?" Trevor asked with a welcoming smile.

"Tall coffee, black." He saw the woman glance his direction. She walked closer to the counter and began looking at the nutrition facts on the back of a granola bar. She took a sip of her drink and immediately spit it out, coughing as the strong mixture made her gag. Nathan and Trevor turned towards her and Trevor laughed. The woman tried to cover her mouth as her eyes watered and she continued coughing.

"Are you alright, ma'am?" Nathan asked, noticing the flush to her cheeks at his unwanted attention. She nodded and attempted to wave off their concern as she turned to regain her composure. When she finally stopped coughing and turned back around, Trevor held out a small cup of water for her and she sipped eagerly.

"I take it the new drink is not a go?" Trevor asked with a teasing tone that made the woman roll her eyes at him. "I'll fix you your usual, Lina."

"Thanks." Her voice was strained as she attempted to recover from her coughing fit.

"You sure you're alright?" Nathan asked again. He waited until her creamy brown gaze found his and she nodded.

"Yes, thank you. Sorry about that unladylike episode." She blushed as she used a napkin to wipe up some of her coffee spit/sludge from the countertop.

He chuckled softly. "No problem."

Trevor handed her a caramel macchiato and swiped a damp rag over the countertop. Nathan saw her gaze wash over him again as he handed a few bills to Trevor. "I have hers too." He nodded towards the woman as he paid for both their drinks.

"Oh, you don't have to do that," she protested, stepping forward and waving away his kindness.

"I know I don't. I want to." His comment caused her to halt her response.

"Well, thank you. I appreciate it." She toasted her cup towards him and cast a wave at Trevor as she stepped away from the counter and towards the door.

"Have fun on your date tonight," Trevor called after her, receiving a wave over her shoulders. Nathan held the door open for her as they both exited and began walking the same direction.

She nodded her thanks again and began to walk ahead of him and stopped. She turned and faced him with a small smile. "You headed this way too?"

He nodded. "That I am."

"I'm going to walk with you," she stated confidently and slid into step beside him. "My name is Evangelina, by the way." She extended her hand.

Nathan smiled and shook it. "Pretty. I'm Nathan."

"Nice to meet you, Nathan."

"You as well. You work around here?"

"Just at the end of the block." She pointed to a tall building on the corner. "You?"

"Across the street from your building it looks like." He pointed to the tall federal building that stood looming across the street, its gray exterior bland and unwelcoming.

"Wow... that looks like a very fun place to work," she teased. "What is that building anyway? I've worked across the street from it for two years and have yet to venture over there and see what it actually is."

"It's a minor field office for the FBI," he responded nonchalantly, as if his job were not intimidating.

Her eyes widened. "FBI? Are you... in the FBI?"

He turned towards her fearful voice and smirked. "Yes. Does that weird you out?"

She tried to mask her surprise and shook her head. "Not at all. I find it... interesting."

He chuckled. "Well, that's good. Most people flee from my presence once they hear I'm an agent."

"Hmm—" she responded thoughtfully. "I think I feel more embarrassed that I didn't realize that the building I stare at most of the day was the FBI."

"To be fair, there's no signage." He pointed out as she accepted that detail in her favor.

Evangelina's cell phone rang and she rolled her eyes. "Sorry, I just need to take this for one sec." She slid her finger over the screen and answered. "Not now, Andy. I already agreed to go on the stupid date, now leave me alone until I see you at lunch." She hung up as quickly as she answered.

"So, I couldn't help overhearing at the coffee shop, and just now, you have a date tonight?"

"Ugh, don't remind me." She blushed under his scrutiny.

"I take it you don't like the guy?"

"Oh, I have no idea. I've never met him."

"A blind date, then?"

"Yes. The seventh one in three weeks."

He grimaced and she nodded in agreement. "I know, right? But my friend thinks I don't put myself out there enough and that I'm destined to be alone unless she intervenes." Her dry commentary made him laugh and received a slight arm slap from her. "Don't laugh. It's awful. It's like speed dating, only instead of a few minutes, I have to spend an entire dinner with them. And oh, it is awful when it's a dinner *and* another activity. So awful."

"What is so bad about them?"

"Besides having to have the same conversation I've had a million times with other blind dates? Everything."

He laughed heartily, his wide smile making her smile in return. "Perhaps the guys just want to make a good impression."

She sent him a doubtful look, which made him smile again, and she smirked as they reached the revolving glass doors of her building. "Well, this is me." She pointed towards the direction she would need to continue to walk. He glanced at the name on the door. "Armm and Goode Publishing. I see. So you are an editor?"

She nodded. "Yes. Good guess."

"It's really the only position I could think of for a publishing company," he admitted and received the light laugh he had hoped she would give.

"Hm, well it was a good guess. I spend most of my days dissecting words, adding in a few anadiplosis, eponyms, or polysyndetons. Or if I'm feeling real adventurous some epizeuxis."

"I have no idea what any of those are." Nathan admitted. "So I'm impressed already."

Laughing, she flashed a friendly smile. "It was nice bumping into you this morning, Agent Nathan."

She held up her cup of coffee. "And thanks for this. I owe you."

"Perhaps you do." His firm gaze held hers until she blushed and glanced away. "Have a good day, Evangelina." He nodded in farewell and continued across the street. He turned at the entry of his building and caught her staring. He flashed one last smile and waved. She gave a quick wave in response as if embarrassed at being caught watching him and darted inside her building.

∞

Nathan rubbed his hand over his face as he waited for the clock to strike five o clock. He glanced at the image on his screen of Evangelina's beautiful face. Her high cheekbones, almond eyes, and lean face made him wish he could find some excuse to visit Armm and Goode Publishing and compare the picture to the original. When he realized how stalkerish his thoughts sounded, he shook his head and glanced at his watch again. A knock on his door frame had his head popping up to see his partner and friend, Special Agent Luke Howard, popping his head into his office. "So, ready for your date tonight?"

"Don't remind me."

"You don't seem so excited. What gives?"

"Because it's a blind date with a woman I don't know," Nathan mumbled. "Although, I will say, I had an interesting encounter with a woman today who is going through the exact thing I am."

"Oh yeah, and what's that?"

"Meddling friends who think we need a love life," Nathan confirmed, causing Luke to throw his head back and laugh. Luke flashed his dimpled smile and his brown eyes sparkled as he combed a hand through his brown hair. "Maybe some of us who have found that special person want others to experience the same happiness."

"Hm, I didn't realize you were seeing someone." Nathan grunted as he briefly turned back to his screen and minimized the website to the publishing house. He powered off his computer and grabbed his car keys. "Well, where am I meeting this woman tonight?"

"I've been seeing someone for three weeks. How have you not known this? I talk about her every day."

"Not to me."

"I call bull on that one, my friend. Maybe you just tune me out because you're afraid the bug might catch."

Nathan's brow narrowed.

"Reservations are at Mode over on Third. They are under my last name. Seven o clock."

"Am I fine wearing this?"

"Really? You're not even going to change?"

"Wasn't planning on it," Nathan added. "By the time I make it to my loft and to the restaurant, I may be late. So, would you rather me be late or wear what I have on?"

Luke groaned. "Alexander, this is why you are still single. Women appreciate the extra mile."

"Who said I didn't want to be single anymore?"

"Trust me, you don't. Not in New York City."

Nathan pondered Luke's comment as his mind wandered to Evangelina again. He glanced at his watch, right on the dot five. Grabbing his suit jacket off the back of his chair, he darted out of his office. "I have to go."

"Don't be late!" Luke called after him.

Nathan exited the building, his eyes flashing across the street and spotting Evangelina heading out of her office building at the same time. She looked up and spotted him, her steps faltering a moment as she waved in his direction. He waited across the street as she crossed the sidewalk. She fell into step beside him. "Fancy meeting you here," she greeted, resituating her purse strap after the man beside her bumped it in passing.

"Indeed," Nathan greeted. "How was your day?"

She sighed. "Long and busy. You?"

"Long... and busy."

She grinned. "Mine is only going to get longer. Blind date number seven tonight."

"I actually understand that frustration."

"You do?"

"Dating, I mean. It's tough."

"Not sure it would be so tough if I actually wanted to do it, but it is what it is, so they say." She smiled as she pointed to the upcoming metro entrance. "That's me."

"Well, this is where I leave you then." He motioned towards the sidewalk stretching past the metro entrance.

A brief disappointment washed over her features, making his pulse quicken at the thought of her wanting to spend more time with him. She quickly masked her feelings and smiled. "Well, I guess I will see you tomorrow morning then, Agent Nathan."

"I look forward to it, Evangelina."

She lightly saluted towards him as she continued on her way down the stairs. "By the way," She paused on the top step, people scurrying passed her as she looked his direction. "it's Lina."

He nodded in understanding as he watched her continue down the steps. He briefly rubbed a hand over his heart and the funny dance he felt in his chest as he made his way towards the bookstore two blocks over to wait until seven to head to Mode Restaurant for the date he now dreaded even more.

Chapter Two

Lina slipped out of her bedroom and grabbed her purse by the front door. She settled upon an emerald green cocktail dress that she paired with nude-colored heels and her charcoal peacoat. Overall, she felt she was dressed up enough for the nice restaurant, but also comfortable. The dress was one of her favorites. And bonus, she reminded herself, she'd purchased it at a discount.

"Wait!" Andy called out and slid across the kitchen in her socks to look and approve Lina's outfit. "Yes, that dress looks great. You look beautiful. Now remember, be nice."

Lina opened her mouth to reply, but Andy halted her words with a wave of her hand. "I'm just saying that because the last two reports I received from the men have said you were not so friendly."

Lina shrugged her shoulders. "Maybe if they didn't freak out over a lost ball game or hit on other women, I'd have a reason to be nicer."

Andy narrowed her gaze until Lina sighed. "Fine. Yes, I will be nice. At least this one is at a good restaurant. I'll see you around nine."

"I hope not. I hope it goes well and you stay out all night. Remember the reservation is under Davenport or Howard," Andy called after her.

Amy walked the couple of blocks over toward Mode and found herself dragging her feet in dread. She was slightly early, but maybe that meant she could grab a glass of wine to relax before meeting Mr. Dud. She entered the restaurant and the perky hostess welcomed her with a smile. "Reservation name?"

"Davenport or Howard, I'm told. I'm not quite sure which."

The girl ran her finger down a ledger and then beamed. "Here you are. Looks like you are the first one here, would you like to be seated or perhaps make a trip to the bar until the rest of your party arrives?"

"The bar will be fine."

"Of course." She escorted Lina to the bar and waited until Lina found a seat at the high counter. The bartender smiled in greeting.

"White wine, please," she requested. He nodded silently and filled a glass with the chilled wine that would no doubt smooth over her rough edges she'd managed to acquire throughout her long day at the office. The manuscripts she'd been working on took turns she hadn't expected, and she'd spent the remainder of her day fleshing out story instead of finalizing projects. She took a long sip relishing the feeling of something cold and crisp.

"Is this seat taken?" She turned to find an older gentleman, pudgy around the middle with a unique balding pattern on his head that looked somewhat like a Rorschach test, expectantly staring at her.

Though she dreaded potential small talk, she waved her hand at the stool. "No. Help yourself."

He slid up onto the stool and flagged the bartender down. "I'll have a scotch, and I would like to order the beautiful lady next to me another wine, please."

Lina accepted the drink politely, but now wished she hadn't as the man began the beginnings of introductions. Lina responded politely to his questions and glanced at her watch. Ten more minutes. *Where was her date? Wait... how was it she had dreaded her date all afternoon, and now she prayed the man would just walk through the door to rescue her from Mr. Balding?*

She felt a hand slide over the small of her back and she straightened immediately at the touch. Turning with appalled curiosity, her gaze softened as she gazed upon none other than Agent Nathan.

"Hey there, Lina." He smiled warmly.

Her jaw dropped as she sat in stunned silence. "Nathan! Hi!" She smiled in relief as he slid onto the stool next to her. "Hello." Nathan reached behind her to shake the other man's hand. The man shook his hand politely and then nodded as if he received the silent signal that Lina belonged to Nathan and he slipped off the stool and walked away. "Did I just ruin the big date?" Nathan grimaced and then winked as Lina giggled.

"No. Unfortunately the date has yet to show up. I'm just waiting in here until he graces me with his presence."

"I see. Well, you look beautiful."

She blushed at his compliment. "Thank you. So, what brings you here?"

The hostess walked up, interrupting his response. "If you two will follow me, I will show you your table."

Lina turned to the woman in surprise. "Oh no, I'm sorry. This is not the man I'm meeting. I'm not quite sure who it will be."

"No ma'am. Reservations for Howard include the both of you." The waitress' brow furrowed as she stared from Lina to Nathan. Nathan wriggled his eyebrows her direction.

"Wait... you're my date?" Lina asked in surprise.

He nodded. "It appears so."

"W-wait... how?"

He laughed and held up his hands and shrugged. "Looks like our friends know one another. Now, may I have the pleasure of your company?"

He extended his hand and Lina slowly eased her hand into his as she grabbed her wine glass and allowed him to thread her arm though his elbow as they followed the hostess to their table. He pulled out her chair and waited for her to sit before rounding the table and doing the same.

Lina watched him carefully as he ordered a glass of wine as well.

"Why do you keep staring at me like that?" he asked.

"Like what?"

"In disbelief." He chuckled as she lightly ran a hand over her flushed cheek.

"I am just surprised. You are not the type of guy Andy normally fixes me up with. How do you know Andy?"

"I don't. I know Luke."

"Luke? Who is Luke?"

"Apparently he and Andy are dating and planned to fix us up on this date. I have to admit, I am not complaining."

She blushed again and inwardly cursed herself for her transparency.

"So, what type of guys does Andy normally fix you up with?" he asked curiously.

She sighed in annoyance. "Oh, you know, the overly eager businessman who loves money. His money, your money, everyone else's money, and only wants more money. Or the over-enthusiastic sports fanatic who completely melts down after a loss. The good ones." Her sarcastic response made him laugh.

"And how do you know I don't want to know about your money?" He winked at her as she grinned.

"True, I don't. But then I would have to burst your bubble and say you are barking up the wrong tree then, because I certainly am not your ticket to a lavish lifestyle."

He laughed again and Lina found herself drawn to the melodic sound and the sparkle in his eyes.

"So I ranted about blind dates this morning and you didn't say a word about your own for this evening. Do you go on blind dates often?" Lina asked, wondering why a gorgeous man like him would even need help in the dating department.

"I was still coming to terms with the idea. And no, actually, this is my first one. I have to say, I feel pretty lucky. I hear blind dates can be nasty little devils."

She chuckled and nodded. "You have no idea."

"So why don't you just tell your friend no?"

Amy shrugged. "Because it is fun for her. She only wants to see me happy and in love. I can't blame her for wanting the best for me. And honestly, I want those things too, I'm just okay with the idea of it taking me a while to reach them."

"You aren't happy now?"

"Oh, I'm happy. I meant... just happy *with* someone as well. Does that make any sense?"

He nodded. "I understand."

"So why did you accept the offer of a blind date? I have to admit, I am crazy curious." She leaned forward in eagerness awaiting his answer resting her chin in her hand.

He smirked and then took a long sip of his wine, watching her over the rim of his glass. "For the same purpose, I guess. Luke is a great guy. I am relatively new to the New York area and he wanted me to meet people... especially women."

"I see. Meet any interesting ones so far?"

"Yes, I have, though nothing to write home about. It's quite a curse on their part that I work for the FBI and am gifted in researching people."

"Stalker," Amy teased.

He shrugged. "I prefer cautious."

"So, have you already researched me and discovered all my secrets?"

"Hardly." He grinned as the waiter walked up and greeted them.

"Good evening, sir. Ma'am." He nodded towards Lina. "What may I order for you?"

Baffled, she realized she hadn't even perused the menu due to being so distracted by Nathan. And he was worth looking at. She liked that his sandy brown hair was slightly overdue for a haircut and brushed the edges of his collar. She also liked his green eyes. They were sharp, focused, and warm when he looked at her. And though she'd only seen him in a suit, when he'd removed his jacket, she liked the outline of his muscular frame as well. She'd yet to find anything wrong with him.

Nathan responded for her. "Sorry, I've been so transfixed on my beautiful date, I have yet to look over the menu. Can you give us a couple minutes?"

The waiter smiled and nodded, slinking back to whatever dark corner he'd occupied prior.

"I guess we better take a peek at the menu." Nathan flipped his open and began looking it over. Lina closed hers quickly and watched him as he studied his. He had slipped on a pair of glasses that she found made him even more appealing than he was before. *Was that even possible?* He caught her eye and his lips tilted ever so slightly. "What'cha thinkin'?"

She grinned as she rested her chin on both of her hands. "Would you be offended if I said I wasn't very hungry?"

He laid his menu down on the table and studied her carefully. "No. Is this you saying you don't want to eat anything?"

"Not exactly," she replied, lifting her menu to face him and then pointed to a lavish piece of chocolate cake that graced the front of the dessert section.

He laughed. "I see. You want chocolate cake, yet you do not want dinner?"

She nodded and lightly nibbled her bottom lip in apprehension that he might think she were weird or rude. Smiling, he slid his hand across the table and squeezed her own before raising his other hand and signaling the waiter. He handed the man their menus. "The lady and I would just like to split that intense slice of chocolate cake you have on the dessert menu."

"Yes sir." The waiter nodded and hurried away.

Lina smiled. "I like your glasses."

"My glasses?" His cheeks flushed as he fumbled with the lenses on his face as if he'd forgotten to remove them before she caught too much of a glimpse of him wearing them.

"Yes. You pull them off well."

"Thanks."

"You're welcome. I think they look... charming," she finished and took another sip of wine.

"Charming, hm? Well perhaps I should wear them more often."

"Perhaps you should."

He avoided her gaze a moment as if he were unaccustomed to such compliments and Lina found the act an appealing one. She added that to the list of his positive attributes.

∞

Her eyes gleamed with interest and Nathan found himself sliding his chair closer to her, sitting next to her instead of across the table. Her eyes widened in surprise at his movement.

"If we are to share a cake, I'd much rather do it from here than across the table. Plus," He leaned closer towards her and sniffed. "You smell lovely."

She blushed as she allowed him to drape his arm over the back of her chair. "So, tell me about yourself, Lina."

"What would you like to know?"

"Anything."

"Well, I work at Armm and Goode Publishing, as you know. I love chocolate and girly coffees and the color green... which means I like your eyes." She nodded towards him and he nodded in thanks to her compliment and smirked. "I like men who drive big trucks, I enjoy late night talk shows, and potato chips. What else would you like to know?"

He laughed. "Very good. Very good. Um... I guess you covered some good ones."

"How about you? Tell me about yourself, Nathan."

He inhaled deeply and sighed as if he were a boring topic. "Well, let's see. I moved here a year ago from Boston. I was stationed at that field office for four years. I have been in New York since then. I am originally from Tennessee, that is where my family continues to live. I like chocolate as well, strong coffee, women who drive reasonable vehicles, late night movies, and greasy hot dogs from the street vendors. Did I cover everything you did?"

"You forgot your favorite color," Lina remarked playfully.

"Ah, blue it is."

"And what do you mean by reasonable vehicle?"

"You know, smart ones that hold more than two people. A woman should drive a car that she can load up her babies in, not some sporty little car that you have to fold yourself into."

Lina laughed. "So, she has to have room for babies?"

"Yes."

She laughed again. "I see."

"What do you drive?"

Lina smirked and then rolled her eyes. "You mean you can't just secret spy type into your phone and find out?"

"No, actually, much to my disappointment."

"Well, when I actually drive, I drive an SUV."

"Ah, a reasonable vehicle. I knew it!"

Laughing, she playfully swatted his arm as the waiter placed their chocolate cake in front of them. Lina grabbed her dessert fork and pinned a small piece of cake. "You get first bite." She held her fork towards him and watched as his lips slid over it to accept the bite. She watched him savor the piece. "Good?"

"Wow." He took a sip of his wine. "That is very rich. Not for the faint of heart."

She forked another piece and took a bite. She rolled her eyes and sighed in pleasure. "Mmmmm. This was a good choice."

They ate several pieces and then Nathan laid his fork down. "Alright, if I keep eating this, I'm going to start craving something salty."

"Likewise. Want to grab a to-go carton? We can go grab some chips or something and finish it in the park?"

Nathan tilted his head at her suggestion. "I like that idea. Let's do it."

He flagged the waiter and settled their bill while accepting the container for Lina to slide their cake into its temporary storage. She then slid her arm in his and let him lead her to the door. "Walk or drive?"

"Walk," Lina answered on a whimsical sigh as she inhaled the scent of the city. "Thank you for today, Nathan."

"Today?"

"Yes. Today. From the nice little meeting at the coffee shop, to walking to work, to a great dinner date... thank you."

"Well, the night is not over. No point in thanking me just yet."

"Oh? You have other great things planned?"

Nathan turned a pointed gaze towards her that made an instant blush cover her cheeks. "Perhaps I do."

Lina walked with him to a small bodega and perused the aisles for the perfect salty treat.

"What do we have here?" Nathan yanked several things from her hands. "Beef jerky, peanuts, and sunflower seeds. Are you secretly a man?"

Lina burst into laughter and clapped him on the back. "No, but I do love snack food. I guess that's another thing you should know about me. I have a snack drawer in my desk at work, and whoa is it overloaded."

He smiled at her as he placed her items in the basket he was carrying.

"Lina?" A man's low baritone voice filtered down the aisle and had Lina turning with an apologetic glance towards Nathan.

"Brett, hello. Good to see you."

The man walked up and eyed her appearance from head to toe and then bounced his gaze to Nathan. "You going to introduce me to your friend?" Brett asked.

"Oh, of course," Lina nervously jittered. "Nathan, this is Brett. Brett, this is Nathan."

"Nice to meet you." Nathan shook his hand and offered a warm smile.

Brett's attention went back to Lina. "So, I left a message with your assistant the other day and never heard back from you."

Nathan felt Lina's grip on his arm tighten slightly as she shifted nervously from one foot to the other. "It's been a busy week at the office. Was it important?"

"Does it matter now? It was Monday when I called, and it is now Friday," Brett answered shortly.

"I guess you're right," Lina replied. "I've sort of been out of pocket at work the last week due to two big projects. Sorry I was not able to return your phone call."

"Phone calls." Brett corrected. "I've called Andy a few times to relay my messages."

"Yes, well, like I said. I've been busy," Lina answered, her voice growing firmer.

"Well, I can see that," Brett combated, eyeing Nathan with disdain. "I guess I wasn't the only man suckered into a blind date. Hey, maybe she won't run out on you like she did me." Brett walked away without a fleeting glance and exited the small store.

"Punk," Lina mumbled under her breath.

"And dare I ask who that man was?" Nathan grimaced.

"That would be the 'I spend time hitting on other women and getting phone numbers while on a date with you' blind date. I'm sorry if that was awkward."

"Not at all." Nathan flashed a quick smile her way and wondered what man wouldn't want to give Lina his full attention during a date.

"I guess, since this happened, I should explain the whole blind date thing."

"You don't have to. You mentioned your friend was setting you up a lot."

"Yes, but I did not tell you I committed to going on ten dates."

"And I'm number seven, right?"

"Yes." She palmed her face in her hand and he grinned, gently pulling it away from her cheek.

"Are you embarrassed?"

"Yes." She flushed as she nervously grabbed another bag of potato chips and placed them in the basket.

"Don't be. It's all good in my book. I wouldn't have met you otherwise."

"That is a false statement. We met this morning, on our own."

"Ah, yes, but then it would have been weeks before I mustered up enough courage to ask you out. Think of all that time wasted."

She smiled in thanks and slipped from his arm to walk down the aisle, her once happy-go-lucky demeanor now mellowed into a morose attitude of defeat.

"Listen, Lina," Nathan called to her as he caught up with her. "How about we wrap this up and take it back to your place or something and watch a late-night show of sorts."

"Really?"

"Yeah, why not? It's getting a bit chilly outside anyway."

"Well, I have a roommate. I will need to call Andy and see if that's okay."

"Fine by me. I'll be eyeing the delectable array of cheese crackers." He watched as she bit back a smile and slipped out her phone.

Chapter Three

"You better not be calling me because you have already left your date. It's only eight o clock."

Lina grinned at her friend's berating attitude. "Actually, my date and I were wanting to come to the apartment and watch some tv while we eat our snacks. Is that okay?"

"Wait... what? You want to bring him *here*? A guy you *just* met? Of course it's okay!" Andy squealed. "Yes! I *knew* it! Luke is here anyway and since you're currently on a date with his friend, that would be fine. And you need to meet him too. I'll tell him. Yay! I'm so glad it's going well."

"Don't get to thinking too crazy of thoughts," Lina teased.

Nathan heard her conversation and he chuckled as she glanced over at him and winked.

"Hey now! I wasn't thinking that!" Andy defended. "Okay, maybe I was a little. But still, hurry up so I can meet this guy!"

Lina hung up and grinned. "It's fine, and apparently your friend Luke is over at my place, so looks like our date may turn into a double date, if that is okay?"

"Fine with me. Now where shall we go?"

"It's actually just several blocks up." Lina unpacked their basket on the counter and the attendant rang up their total. "I've got this." Lina placed her hand on top of Nathan's as he went to hand his card to the cashier. "You bought dinner. I'll buy this."

"Dinner was a piece of chocolate cake," Nathan replied as he nodded for the cashier to accept his card.

Lina blew a frustrated breath. "Fine, but I get it the next time."

"Next time? Ah, well I like the sound of that." Nathan pocketed his wallet and grabbed their bag. Lina felt his hand at the small of her back as he escorted her out of the store. "Did you drive to the restaurant?"

"No, actually. I took the metro," Nathan answered.

"Well, I walked as well, so it looks like we will have a small trek, if that is alright?"

"Time with you, Evangelina, I am definitely okay with."

"I will admit this evening has gone better than I imagined it would."

"Yeah?"

"You were a nice surprise." She looked up at him and the streetlights brightened his green gaze. They walked in silence for a few minutes and made their way to her apartment complex, the older building graced with wrought iron balcony rails and an elderly doorman.

"Good evening, Thomas," Lina greeted the man.

"Well good evening, Ms. Harper. How are you?" He opened the door and eyed Nathan with a protective eye. Nathan nodded in greeting.

"I'm wonderful. Tell Patsy I said hello," Lina called over her shoulder as they made their way to a stairwell, avoiding the elevator. She smiled as they made their way to door number 432. Sliding her key in the lock, she opened the door, and walked inside. "Hey, hey, hey!" she called out.

Andy, a petite, blonde headed woman with bright blue eyes rounded the corner. Her face spread into a wide smile as she openly checked Nathan out. "Well, look who it is. How was the blind date?" She asked with a knowing grin.

Lina rolled her eyes and laid her bag on the counter. "The date is great, and still going, so make yourself scarce."

Nathan laughed as he lightly placed a hand at the small of Lina's back and stepped forward, extending his hand towards Andy.

"Hi, my name is Nathan Alexander."

Andy's smile widened and she pumped his hand vigorously. "Nice to meet you. Andy Waterstone."

"Alexander?" Lina asked, turning towards him.

He nodded.

"I like it," she complimented, as she reached into their bag and grabbed their slice of cake and snacks.

"So where is this Luke guy?" Lina asked.

Andy blushed. "Oh... he's... in the shower."

Lina and Nathan both looked at her in surprise. "In the shower?" they said in unison.

Andy nodded. "I sort of spilled spaghetti sauce... all over him." She motioned her hands over her middle.

Lina and Nathan burst into laughter.

"Hey now, don't make fun," Andy scolded, but she wore a small smirk. "So, how was dinner?"

"It was good. This is what we ordered, and we are going to finish it." Lina held up the slice of chocolate cake and sat on a stool at the bar. She toasted her fork with Nathan's as they dug into the slice. Andy filtered through their grocery bag and she cringed. "Seriously, Lina? You took the man snack shopping?"

"Hey!" Lina grabbed the bag from her roommate's hands and brought it to her lap. "That's part of our dinner as well."

"Dinner? You went to Mode and only ordered chocolate cake?" Andy scolded Lina with her gaze. Andy turned towards Nathan. "Sorry, Nathan. My friend here loves to just snack in the evenings, she never eats. If you would like some real food, I have some spaghetti left."

"Actually, I find this dinner quite delightful, but thank you, Andy." Nathan smiled at Lina and then gently dabbed his napkin over her bottom lip, holding the frosting-stained napkin up for her to see. She chuckled as she covered her mouth on her next bite.

"It's so good," Lina mouthed to Andy.

"I bet it is," Andy mumbled, watching Nathan and Lina watch each other as they ate.

"Well, I am going to bring out some bowls for your snacks. Was Petra working?"

"No, I think this person was new. Oh, and by the way, Brett was there."

Andy cringed. "Eesh, how'd that go? Wait, should we be talking about this in front of... number seven?" She muttered at the end and had Nathan bursting into laughter.

"I already know about the ten blind dates, so don't tiptoe around me, please."

"You told him?" Andy asked in surprise.

"I wanted to be honest. Besides, we met this morning before our actual date, so..."

Andy waved her hand in excitement. "Hold the phone. No way! How? When?"

At Trevor's Coffee House," Lina explained.

"Though we walk the same route to work every day." Nathan added.

"And how have I not seen you before?" Lina asked, turning back towards him.

"Probably because I enjoy walking behind you."

She gaped and then flushed as he winked at her.

"Well, I'm glad you two have hit it off. I had to at least get one right."

"It's great to see you like her," a deep voice rang out as Luke strutted into the room shirtless and confident. Lina noted the slight pink tinge to Andy's cheeks as she spotted him, and Lina tilted her head and openly surveyed his firm set of abs.

"You must be Lina." Luke extended his hand and grinned.

"Yes. You must be Mr. Dreamboat."

He laughed. "I hope so."

"Nice to meet you." Lina reached and grabbed a beef jerky and opened it, snapping it in half and handing a piece to Nathan. He grinned as he accepted it and took a hearty bite, yanking it in his teeth to break a piece off. Lina giggled and did the same.

"So weird," Andy mumbled as she poured herself a glass of wine. "So, Luke, apparently we did not set up a blind date. They already knew one another."

Luke stepped forward in disappointment. "You did?"

"It was still a surprise." Nathan spoke towards Andy. "I had no idea I would be bumping into this beautiful woman tonight and be so lucky to have her on my arm. Fate had other plans though." He lightly brushed his fingers over Lina's hand before giving it a squeeze.

Luke glanced at his watch. "Wow, is that the time? Alexander, we better jet."

"I'm still on my date."

"Yeah, but we have to wake up in about four hours. Don't you want some sleep?" Luke asked with concern.

Lina turned towards Nathan. "You didn't tell me you had an early morning. You should go and get some rest before you have to work."

He shook his head. "I will be fine."

"Nathan," Lina and Luke stated at the same time.

Nathan chuckled. "Oh, alright. If you're going to team up on me, I guess I will leave."

He stood and accepted the hand Lina offered as she walked him towards the door. Luke followed closely behind, freshly showered and pulling on what she knew could not be his shirt as it was a couple of sizes too small. Lina opened the door and Luke walked out and waited for Nathan to follow. Lina shut the door at Luke's retreating back as they heard him object on the other side.

"You shutting him out?" Nathan asked in amusement.

"Well, I wanted to finish my date how I wanted to," Lina answered defiantly. "This is where I say I had a great time. I'm glad it was you that showed up at Mode and not the bald guy. Thanks for eating cake with me... and beef jerky." She grinned up at him as he gently brushed her hair aside and behind her ear. Surprisingly, she didn't mind the contact.

"I would like to see you again." Nathan ran his hand down her arm to her hand and linked his fingers with hers. "And not just at the crosswalk, if that's alright?"

"I'd like that." Lina inhaled a deep breath as she watched him tug his phone out of his pant pocket. "May I have your number, Evangelina?"

She rambled off her phone number.

"There. There you are under 'Beautiful Blind Date'." He showed her his screen and she laughed.

"Awesome. Well, be careful tomorrow, with whatever you have to do."

"Boring stuff, I assure you."

"I highly doubt that, Agent Nathan."

He flashed his charming smile and Lina felt her knees go weak as he reluctantly released her hand and opened her door to an annoyed Luke who stood leaning against the opposite wall of the hallway with his arms crossed. She offered him a brief wave before closing the door behind Nathan.

"Whoa, Whoa, Whoa!" Andy squealed. "What the what was that?!"

Lina ran a hand over her flaming cheeks. "I have no idea, but Nathan is... great."

"Um, apparently."

"Is it crazy that I cannot wait to see him tomorrow, and I'm dying to text him right now?"

Andy squealed again just as Lina's cell phone buzzed with an incoming text message. Lina's face lit up when she saw it was not a number she recognized. "I think it's him." She opened the text and she did a small jig.

Nathan: *"This morning I thought I had met the most beautiful woman I had ever seen. This evening I found that to be true. Had fun today and tonight. Thinking of you now. – Nathan"*

"Well, what did he say?" Andy prodded eagerly.

Lina read her the text message and Andy beamed. "Yay! Looks like lucky number seven is the winner! Ding, ding, ding!"

"I did tell him I committed to ten blind dates," Lina replied.

"And you're still willing to go on them after *that*?"

"If you want me to," Lina agreed. "I told you I would, so I will."

"Well, I want you to, but I'm not sure the remaining guys could even compete with that hottie. Besides, he works with Luke, which means he's an agent, which is kind of sexy if you think about it."

"I will admit he intrigues me." Lina ran a hand through her hair. "I think I'm going to end my night on a good note and shower. I am one tired lady."

"Alright. Well, sweet dreams," Andy called after her in a sing song voice that had Lina laughing.

"Indeed, my friend! Indeed!"

∞

"So..." Luke began as he peered through his binoculars at the abandoned warehouse near the bridge. "You thinking of pursuing Lina?"

"I think I would be a complete fool if I didn't. I'm still a bit annoyed our date was cut short due to this," Nathan answered, also watching the warehouse closely. "Also, I found out her previous blind date was Brett Richeson."

Luke lowered his binoculars and turned to his partner in shock. "What?"

"Yeah, apparently he took her on a date and she ended up leaving in the middle of it."

"You think she knows anything?"

"I don't know. She seemed quite annoyed with him. If she knew of any of his illegal activities, then I think she would have acted differently."

"Well, that is an interesting twist for sure. Maybe it is a good thing for you to get close to her. The closer you are to her, the closer you are to Brett Richeson."

"I don't think so." Nathan shifted in his seat to stretch his legs a bit in the small sedan. "If anything, you should see what Andy knows about him. She's the one that set the date up."

"Good call. From what I gather they went to college together, and he's new to the city."

"You should see what all he told Lina about himself on their date."

Nathan grunted. "I don't want to pursue her for only work reasons. I actually like the woman. She's spunky and quirky and beautiful. And the last thing I want to do is bring up another guy she went out with in the same fashion she did me. Besides, from what I've heard so far, there wasn't much of a date. Lina left in the middle of it."

"I'm just saying she may be a good source or even a chip in the game later on. Valuable."

"Yes, well, I would like to think it won't come to that. No word to the SAC about this. If she finds out the woman I'm dating is connected to a possible source in the Gibson case, she'll have me pick Lina apart, and that would completely ruin any chance I have at dating her."

"Understood," Luke replied as he spit a sunflower seed out the open window.

"So, what about you and Andy?" Nathan prodded.

Luke shrugged and lifted his binoculars again. "She's cool. We've been friends for a while, it's just recently been where we have had the opportunity of hanging out more."

"She's pretty as well."

"She is," Luke agreed. "But I'm not looking for something long term right now."

"You said you'd found someone special." Nathan reminded him.

"She is. Doesn't mean I want something long term at the moment."

Is that what she's looking for? Long term?"

"I have no idea. I haven't asked. But with this Gibson investigation going on, I don't have the time to dedicate to dating anyone right now. It wouldn't be fair to her."

"Yet you've been seeing her for a few weeks."

"When I can, yes. I like the possibility of long-term, I'm just trying to remain realistic."

"You saying I'm not being realistic in wanting something with Lina?"

"No, that's not what I'm saying. I know enough about Lina from Andy to know she is independent enough to handle your busy schedule. Andy... well, she's a different story. She demands time, and she deserves it. I just can't commit to that sort of demand just yet. But I'm definitely interested."

"Hmm..." Nathan quietly responded as he watched a black sedan pull up to the warehouse and Peter Gibson stepped out and glanced around. Luke quickly raised his camera and zoomed in on Gibson's face and took several shots, and more shots of the vehicle and license plate. Another man appeared in the doorway of the warehouse. "Who are you?" Nathan whispered as he continued to study the scene through his binoculars.

Luke's cell buzzed and he quickly snatched it up to see who the text was from. "It's Andy."

"You can talk to your girlfriend later," Nathan mumbled as he began taking photos of the second man.

"It's about you," Luke baited. He noted the slight rise in Nathan's brow and took that as a 'please continue' sign.

"Apparently Lina has been on cloud nine since your date tonight. Andy said she was even humming in the shower, and she *never* hums in the shower. 'NEVER' being spelled in all caps," Luke chuckled. "What did you do to the woman, Alexander?"

Nathan flashed him an innocent smile. "Is it hard to believe I'm charming?" He cranked the engine on their car to head back to headquarters, pleased with the surprising events of the day.

Chapter Four

Lina yawned at her desk and lightly typed up her report for the McCullough manuscript. She'd actually enjoyed the work. The historical fiction novel had her traveling through turn of the century England following a female sleuth bent on solving a murder and finding love along the way. She'd spent two months poring over the manuscript to fine tune it for her boss. Now it was time to pass it on. Her desk phone rang, and she pressed the speaker phone button. "Evangelina Harper," she greeted.

"Ms. Harper, you have a visitor."

"Alright." Curious, Lina straightened her blouse. "Send them in."

A knock sounded on her office door and her assistant, Asa, flashed an amused smile. "Right this way." He motioned inside her office and a quartet of plaid-clad doowop singers walked inside. They immediately began serenading her and ended with singing a dinner invitation to a small restaurant and club in East Village for seven that evening. She agreed, amused that Nathan would send such an invite. She laughed as the gentlemen left and Asa stood to the side in wonder. "What on Earth, Lina?"

"Just a…" She waved her hand towards the door. "A silly invite, that's all."

"But you like it," Asa pointed out and then his eyes widened. He hurried inside her office and shut the door behind him, plopping down into one of the purple chairs across from her desk. "Wait, are these from the blond man from the other day?"

Her answering flush had him bouncing his legs. "No way! That's great. So, who is he? What's his name?"

A knock sounded on her door again and Asa answered briskly. One of the front secretaries, eyeing Asa with disdain at having to cater to his supervisor instead of him doing so, carried a large bouquet of bright flowers. "These came for you, Ms. Harper."

Asa intercepted them and shut the door behind the woman. He spun around. "A singing-graham *and* flowers? What did you do to the poor man?"

She laughed. "I guess he had a good night too." A large smile bloomed over her face as she pointed towards the table by the window. "They're beautiful, aren't they? Let me see the card."

He handed the small white envelope to her. She eagerly opened it and her smile widened when she saw Nathan's name scrolled across the bottom. She then read his note.

"I can't believe I'm sending you flowers after one day of knowing you. This is out of character for me, Evangelina. I hope you smile and think of me." – Nathan

Lina bit her bottom lip as she contained an excited squeal. "Thank you, Asa."

He waved for her to provide more details, but she shook her head. "I don't want to jinx it yet. Now, if you don't mind, I'm going to head out to lunch early."

"No problem. I will hold all your calls."

"Thanks." She grabbed her purse and quickly made her way to the elevator. She grabbed her phone and pondered texting Nathan. She stepped out into the sunlight and glanced towards Nathan's office building. She wondered if she could just show up over there. How did that work? Would she be searched? Would the door even be unlocked for outsiders? Her curiosity won out and she made her way across the street. She walked into the stark marble foyer, void of décor and people, minus one security guard at the security walk through. She placed her bag inside a plastic bin and shoved it through the machine as she stepped through the medal detecting doorway. The agent waved a wand over her body and then waved her through.

"May I help you?" he asked, his broad stance and firm gaze caused Lina to shift in nervousness. The man was probably paid to make people feel uncomfortable. His piercing gaze did the trick.

"Um... hi." She flashed a nervous smile. "If I am wanting to speak to one of your agents, how do I go about doing that?"

The man shifted his weight to his other leg. "Depends. Are you seeking help? Are you providing information on an open investigation? Or are you wanting to set up a meeting?"

"Um, no. Actually, I was hoping to take him to lunch."

She saw the small twitch to his lips as he hid a smile. "I see. The name?"

"Evangelina Harper," she replied, placing a hand over her chest to calm her heart rate.

"No ma'am. The agent's name," he corrected, this time not hiding his smile.

She blushed in embarrassment and smiled nervously. "Oh, right. Nathan Alexander."

"Give me a minute. You can wait over there." He pointed to some chairs near the entry. She nodded and walked over and sat. *Was she making a mistake? Was it too soon to just show up at his work to ask him to lunch?* She didn't know. It'd been a while since she'd wanted to make this sort of effort.

"Lina?" She heard her name and glanced up as Nathan walked down the marble stairway and a large smile spread over his face. He wore slacks and a crisp button up shirt, but still appeared relaxed, despite his gun holster strapped around his shoulders. He carried a suit jacket in his hands. She couldn't help but smile at him. "What are you doing here?" He kissed her cheek lightly and softly clasped her hands. "I came by to see if you would like to grab lunch."

Nathan's gaze searched her nervous brown eyes. "Of course. This is a nice surprise. I wasn't expecting you."

"And I was not expecting flowers." She softly nudged him.

Laughing, he turned to the security guard. "Clock me out, Thames. I'm heading to lunch with a beautiful woman."

The other agent nodded and watched them leave.

"Is Thames always so tense?" Lina asked.

"He's meant to look intimidating, but underneath he is a softy."

She smiled thinking about the small twitch to the man's lips when she gave him her name instead of Nathan's. "I could see that."

"So where were you thinking of going?" Nathan asked her.

She shrugged. "I honestly hadn't thought that far ahead just yet. I was too busy talking myself into actually walking into your building. It's quite daunting."

Laughing, Nathan draped his arm over her shoulders and pulled her towards him as they walked. "I'm glad you mustered up the courage. I'm starving. Luke and I just got back from assignment."

"Your early morning?" she asked.

"Yes. Just consumed coffee to keep us alert, so I'm running on low, almost E."

"And I didn't exactly feed you a feast last night, either. I bet you are starving. So, what is your favorite thing to eat when you are super hungry?"

"You up for eating outside?" he asked.

"Sure."

"Then let's grab some hot dogs and head to the park. The sun's out so it's not as cold as last night."

"A street hot dog?"

"Is that alright?"

"It's more than alright. That sounds amazing."

He laughed and hugged her closer to him a moment before pointing to his favorite cart a couple of blocks up the street.

∞

"Want to tell me how a little bitty thing like you can down two jumbo dogs?" Nathan asked, impressed that Lina could eat the same amount as himself.

"I was hungry," Lina admitted. "I may regret it later, because I won't be hungry for dinner, but hey, there's always chocolate cake again."

He grinned. "That there is."

"So, what do you do as an agent?" Lina asked.

"Oh, a little bit of this, a little bit of that."

"Is that a way for you to tell me you can't talk about it?"

"Somewhat. Though I mostly look into cybercrimes. We haven't quite caught all the people involved in my current investigation, though we know who most of the key players are. We have to catch them in the act of a few things before we can officially make the arrests."

"Wow." She looked intrigued. "That sounds complicated."

"It can be, especially when you have a lot of little guys working for the big guy. Ideally, you want the big guy, but catching some of those little guys sure feels good too."

He noticed her studying his face. "What?" He swiped a hand over his mouth as if to wipe away any remaining mustard from his lunch.

She tugged his hand down. "Stop. You don't have anything on your face. I was just—" Her lips twitched. "Looking at you."

"Oh." He felt his cheeks warm and hers did the same as she avoided his gaze a brief moment.

"I'm impressed with what you do. Sounds scary, but impressive."

"Thanks."

"Does this mean you're a computer whiz? If you look into cybercrimes?"

"I'm not bad." He grinned as she stood to her feet, glancing at her watch. He followed suit and they began the walk back to their offices.

"I hate that my lunch hour is already almost over. It's been a while since I've branched out. I typically meet Andy at a little sandwich shop up the street. A street hot dog was a nice change."

"I'm glad. I'm still in shock you actually came into my building to ask me."

She bit back a smile. "Tell Thames he's doing a wonderful job up front scaring people away. I almost bolted. My heart was beating so fast." She mimicked its rhythm on her chest.

He laughed. "He'll appreciate that." He opened the door to her building and followed her inside. "Mind if I walk you to your office?"

"Not at all. Only fair." She punched the arrow on the elevator, and they waited as several other men and women gathered around. "My office is on the twenty-third floor. The other floors are other businesses."

They stepped into the elevator, slowly stepping closer and closer as more people filled the tiny space. He could smell her perfume and found himself stepping closer without the help of the other people in the confined space. Her fingers brushed his hand, and he tangled his own with hers as they watched the floor numbers tick by. When they reached her floor, she cut through the remaining people and stepped into a crowded, cubicle-filled office space. "I'm over there." She pointed towards an office across the room and he followed behind her. A man in his early twenties hopped to his feet at the sight of her and stepped forward. "Ms. Harper," he greeted. "You have three messages. I left them on your desk."

"Thank you, Asa." She smiled in thanks as she opened her office door and led Nathan into her own personal space. It was full of bright and cheerful colors and he noticed the flower bouquet he'd sent sitting on her windowsill.

"Let's see—" He leaned towards her window and pulled a blind down to peek through. "Ah, you face my building."

"I do." She grinned.

"Come here." He waved her over and she looked out the window. "See the double doors?"

"Yes."

"Go up eight floors and two windows to the left. That's my office."

"Really?" She pulled the string and raised the blinds to get a better look. "How about that? We've faced each other all this time. Makes you wonder who else hides away in offices all day and we may never know them."

"I'm just glad I met you." Nathan tugged on her hair. "Unfortunately, I should head back."

Disappointment settled over her features and he wished he could sweep her away for the rest of the day. What he'd take her to do, he hadn't the faintest idea, he just wanted to spend more time with her. She walked with him to the elevator, Asa hot on her heels. Nathan looked at the man as he was about to say goodbye to Lina, wondering why the guy hovered so much.

"I'll see you at dinner?" she asked.

His brow rose. "I like the sound of that."

"Seven? Right?"

"Seven is great. I'll be there."

She stepped towards him with a beaming smile. "I can't wait." She kissed his cheek before the doors swung open and he stepped into the elevator. He punched the lobby option and gave one last little wave to her as the doors closed. Dinner at seven, he would definitely be there.

Chapter Five

Date #8

Lina sat at the small table set for two, the comedy club boasting numerous couples settled into their chairs and eagerly awaiting the show that was about to commence. It was an interesting choice for dinner, but the singing-graham sent by Nathan to her office had named this location for seven o' clock. She was a little early and sipped on a glass of white wine as she waited for him to arrive. She eyed the menu, nothing quite catching her eye, as she was still full from the two hot dogs she'd eaten at lunch. But the appetizers looked promising.

"An early bird, I see." A man's voice interrupted her perusal and she glanced up to find a man she didn't know standing next to her table. He pulled out the chair opposite her and sat, already shedding his coat.

"I'm sorry," She waved him to stop. "that seat is saved."

He flashed a quick grin. "I know. I saved it." He extended his hand. "Charlie Poppins—and yes, that's my real name." He gave a small chuckle, his friendly demeanor making her smile.

"You mean you sent the dinner invitation?"

"The singing quartet? Yes. That was me. I know, I know, a little over the top for a blind date, but I thought it would be funny, which—" He waved his hand to encompass the comedy club. "would be a good indicator of where I planned to take you. Too over the top?" he asked.

Baffled that she'd gotten it wrong, she only smiled and shook her head. "No. Clever. Extremely clever. I'm Lina." She shook his hand. "Would you just excuse me for one second?" She stood and walked towards the ladies' room at a hurried pace, fishing in her purse for her cell phone, only it wasn't there. She dug through the various small pockets and realized it must be in her jacket on the back of her chair. She nibbled her bottom lip, trying to think of some way to send an SOS to Andy and an apology to Nathan, who she could only assume was showing up at her apartment any minute expecting dinner, and she was at a comedy club with a complete stranger. She fanned her face as she paced, trying to calm her nerves. Would he be mad? Would this incident ruin her shot with Nathan? She hoped not, but she would definitely be upset if someone stood her up for another date. "Okay," She looked in the mirror, her hands resting on the side of the sink. "get it together, Lina. Just shoot a quick text to Andy and tell her what happened, she can relay the message to Luke, who can then tell Nathan. Or just text Nathan directly. Simple." She inhaled a deep breath, smoothed her hands over her hair and walked back towards her table. She fished in her coat pockets as her date, Charlie, she reminded herself, ordered them an appetizer. No phone. She must have left it at her office. Her heart hammered in her chest at the horrible start to her evening.

"Everything alright?" Charlie asked. His gaze concerned as he studied her.

"Oh, I just forgot my cell phone at the office."

"Ah, I hate when that happens. If you'd like, we can go by there after the show?"

She waved away the offer. "No, that's alright. It'll be fine. Just threw me for a loop is all."

"I understand. Man, I'm attached to this thing." He pulled his from his own pocket. "I left it on the subway a couple of weeks ago and about lost my mind. Thankfully, a nice guy found it and called my roommate. Can you believe that? In New York City? I was shocked."

"That is pretty amazing," she admitted and felt her shoulders relax. Charlie had an easy way about him that settled her nerves. There was nothing she could do in the moment due to her phone being MIA. She could only deal with the here and now. And it would be rude of her to leave Charlie hanging on the account of her own blunder. She wasn't clear enough with Andy about the remaining dates. She didn't realize they were still scheduled as planned. And she hadn't exactly said she no longer wanted to participate, in fact, she told Andy she committed to ten and was going through with them. But her mind had changed after Nathan, why hadn't she just accepted that, and said no more. Then she wouldn't be sitting here, across from a kind and friendly man, thinking about another man, who she'd completely misled into thinking they had dinner plans.

The curtain opened and a spotlight shined on a woman at a microphone. No sense in beating herself up any longer. The situation was what it was, and it just needed to play out. She'd handle the aftermath when she got home. Charlie toasted his glass to hers as the show began to start and Lina gave him a reassuring smile as they watched the comedians deliver a flawless and funny show.

∞

Nathan tapped a knuckle against Lina's apartment door, music blared on the other side, and he felt the thump of the bass against the wood. The door swung open, the loud jams pouring out as a surprised Andy, her hair wrapped up in a bandana, held the vacuum cleaner in one hand, and a dusting cloth in the other. Her eyes widened in surprise. She reached towards a remote and aimed it at the stereo system, turning off the music. "Nathan, wow, this is a surprise." She waved him inside. "What are you doing here?"

He glanced around expecting to see Lina emerge at any moment. "Um, Lina said seven for dinner."

Andy's eyes widened. "Um... Lina isn't here. She's on a date."

"A date?" he asked.

"Yeah. Blind date number eight."

He looked confused.

"She said dinner tonight?" Andy asked him.

"Yes. I assumed here."

She grimaced. "Sorry, she accepted the dinner invitation from Charlie earlier today."

"Charlie." He hadn't meant to say the man's name with such disdain, but his disappointment was palpable.

"You know what, let me shoot her a text. She may have forgotten."

"I don't think she would have forgotten. We talked about it at lunch today."

"You two had lunch together? Well, that would explain her ditching my invite." Andy grinned as she grabbed her cell and texted a quick message to Lina.

A phone dinged on the small table by the door as Lina's phone screen lit up.

"Uh oh. She forgot her phone." Andy shook her head in dismay. "I'll text Charlie."

"No." Nathan halted her. "Don't interrupt the guy's date by saying another guy showed up looking for Lina."

"Okay, well I'll have him tell her about her phone then. She's probably freaking out trying to think where she left it." Andy sent a message and a few seconds later a reply came through.

"Yep, he said she was a bit annoyed at leaving her phone at her office. Guess she forgot she buzzed home to change right quick." Andy set her phone on the counter. "Sorry you're the odd man out tonight."

"Yeah, me too." Annoyance had him stepping back towards the door and running a hand through his hair. "Well, thanks for letting me know."

"I'll tell her to call you."

"If she wants." He walked down the hall, Andy watching him storm away. He didn't wait for the elevator but instead took the stairs. Maybe it was just a misunderstanding. Maybe Lina meant to say tomorrow for dinner. And she hadn't told him she'd decided to still go on the remaining blind dates Andy had planned. He thought she was going to stop after they'd had such a great time together. His mistake on assuming that. And that aggravated him even more.

He hit the street level and passed the doorman Lina had greeted the other night. He offered a forced smile as he headed towards a pizza joint one block over. He'd grab a bite there and then hit the metro to head home.

He surfed his phone. Made some calls. Ate some good pizza and then found himself walking through the subway tunnels completely turned around because his mind was elsewhere. He despised the subway. Yes, it served a valuable purpose in the city, but the smells, the crowds, the suffocating sense that everyone in the city huddled together, had him wishing he'd just walked the few miles home.

He glanced up at the screen to grasp his current location and realized he'd missed his train and would have to wait a while, or he could grab the train headed in the direction he'd just come for a couple of blocks and then intersect his train at that station. He'd do that. He was ready to be moving and not standing still. He hopped onto the train headed back towards Lina's street and held onto the metal bar above his head. The train jolted, his feet shifting to find grip against the floor as it soared through the tunnel. It lurched to a stop at the next stop, and he waited as people flooded in and out of the train car. The doors closed and he surveyed the new faces. His eyes froze when he spotted Lina on the other side of the car. He moved forward through the crowd at a slow pace so he wouldn't lose his grip as the subway made its way towards the next destination. Lina held onto one of the rubber handholds, but the subway's momentum sent her swinging as her heels slipped. He reached her in time for her to slam into his chest. She gasped and glanced up in apology, her face shocked to see him. "Nathan." Breathless, her hand gripped the front of his shirt as she tried to regain her footing. He helped stabilize her and she flushed at her unladylike spin. "I'm so sorry about that."

He couldn't help but smile, because despite his disappointment in her going on another blind date— which he'd finally convinced himself didn't bother him, though it really did— he still liked her.

"I-I was going to call you. When I got home. I left my phone there. I didn't realize—" Her words trailed off as she placed a hand to her forehead. "I am so sorry about tonight. I thought you were my date tonight."

His confusion must have shown because she continued explaining about a singing-gram invitation right before her flower delivery and that she thought he'd sent the gram as well.

"So, you just went on a date with a man you thought was going to be me?"

"Yes. I mean, he was so nice I felt bad once I was there. I didn't want to abandon him there. He'd gone through so much trouble with the invitation that I felt like I had to stick it out. But I did not mean to mislead you. I hope you aren't upset with me."

He chuckled. "You sat through an entire comedy show with another blind date?"

"I did. It wasn't terrible," she admitted. "The show, I mean. Well, and the date. He was nice. Not my type, but nice."

"Should I be relieved?"

She flushed, realizing she'd just shared thoughts she'd normally reserve for Andy.

"Oh, um, I don't know. I just—" She covered her face with her free hand. "I'm sorry, I'm just so embarrassed."

"Don't be. I see now how it was confusing. I will admit, when I showed up at your apartment to a stunned Andy, I was extremely disappointed in the night's events. But hearing that you thought I was the one who'd invited you, and that you would have shown up, makes me feel a little better."

She smiled up at him as the subway came to another stop and she bumped into him. He rested a hand on her hip as a new wave of people began flooding the train. A group of rowdy teens bustled in around them, pushing them closer together. Lina's free hand gripped his arm as the cart took off. The teens began tossing around a cell phone and horse-playing keep away from one of their friends. They bumped into Lina and then Nathan, and the phone continued to hop around the car. They were noisy and boisterous, and the phone soared until it thumped into the side of Nathan's temple. "Alright, alright, enough," Nathan called to the boys. "Save it for outside."

One of the boys popped the collar on his jacket as he tilted his chin in the air and then spit on the floor. "What's this? Some collar junkie thinks he can tell us what to do?"

"Collar junkie?" Nathan looked at Lina. "That's a new one."

She didn't smile as he felt her tuck herself closer to him in nervousness as the boys circled around them. The boy, no older than seventeen, shoved Nathan's shoulder, hoping to knock him off balance, but Nathan stood his ground. Lina gasped as two more boys began teaming up with their friend and eyeing them with contempt.

"Let it be, boys. Let it be," Nathan warned, holding up a hand as a peace offering. The instigator swatted his hand aside and threw a quick punch that connected with Nathan's jaw. Lina, horrified, ducked her head to avoid the next punch from one of the friends.

Nathan growled, as he shoved Lina behind him and caught the next fist in his hand. He took two punches to the ribs as he shoved one kid back onto his rear. They tugged on his jacket, one of his sleeves ripping. People scurried away from the fight to the other side of the train car. Lina stood still, watching in horror as if she didn't want to leave him but didn't know what to do. One boy pulled Nathan's jacket collar behind him, stripping the coat down to his elbows and locking his arms behind him. His gun holster, strapped around his shoulders, made the boys' eyes widen. Two backed off realizing he was law enforcement, but the thug who'd initiated the fight only grew worse. He charged towards Nathan, Nathan bracing himself for the weight, but Lina stepped in front of him, the boy pulling up fast and slipping onto his rear at the sight of her. Her face, hard and upset, stared down at the boy. "How *dare* you." She took a step towards the boy and he looked up in shock as this brave woman towered over him shaking her high heel in his face. "Do not touch him again. Get up," she ordered. The boy continued to sit. "Get up!" she yelled, and the boy scurried to his feet. His friends stood to the side, minding their own business, but transfixed upon Lina's face. "You have ten seconds to get off this train before he calls for backup." She tilted her head towards Nathan, the evidence of him being law enforcement hard to deny. "When those doors open, you better run."

The train jolted to a stop and the doors opened, the boys frozen in shock. "Move!" Lina tossed a thumb towards the door and all the teens rushed out, pushing against one another to escape. Her shoulders relaxed as she turned to face Nathan. "Oh, Nathan." She cupped his face, swelling already appearing on his jaw and blood trickling from his nose.

"I'm fine. Just a little sting."

"Come to my place. We'll clean it up." She reached into her purse and fetched a tissue, lightly dabbing at his split lip. He flinched and gently pulled her hand away from his face.

"I'm fine, Lina."

"I can't believe they did that. Come on." She pulled him towards the doors as they opened at her station. They wound their way through the tunnel and up the steps to street level and walked the half block towards her apartment complex at a hurried pace.

Chapter Six

Thomas, the doorman, greeted them with caution at the sight of Nathan's face, but he held the door for them as Lina led the way to the elevator. She pressed the button several times as if to hurry it along. Turning, she eyed Nathan with pity as bruises began to color his jaw. When the doors opened, she pulled him inside and began dabbing his cut again. He tugged her hand down and smiled, cringing when he did. "I'm fine," he assured her.

"You are not fine. You're bleeding."

She clucked over him a bit more and when they reached her floor, she unlocked the apartment door and pulled him inside, calling for Andy. Her friend's head popped up from the couch, followed by Luke's.

Lina paused. "Whoa. Am I interrupting something?" Lina's smile turned goofy as she watched her friend scramble to her feet.

"No. We were just watching a movie." Andy pointed to the television as a commercial for sports socks flashed across the screen. Luke stood to his feet and nodded in agreement.

"I'll pretend to believe you." Lina tilted her head towards Nathan, the two friends' eyes popping as they saw his bloody lip and bruised face.

"What happened?" Luke asked.

"Did Charlie do this?" Andy asked in shock.

"No. Some boys on the subway."

"The subway?" Andy and Lina nudged Nathan onto a bar stool, as Lina rushed towards the bathroom for a first aid kit. Andy held a washcloth under cold water and brought it over to dab at his lip. He attempted to pull away from her grasp, but she tsked her tongue in response. Lina's voice carried into the room.

"They were rough housing and tossing a phone around and it hit Nathan."

"A phone did that?" Luke's disbelief was evident.

"No," Lina continued. "Their fists did. Nathan told them to cool it, and they got mad."

"So they punched you?" Andy leaned back to look him over.

"More than once," Lina added, as she flipped the lid on the box and removed a disinfectant wipe and nudged Andy's washcloth aside. She dabbed Nathan's lip and he hissed. Her eyes poured into his as he watched her hover over him.

"I'd hate to see the other guy," Luke teased.

"He's fine," Nathan grumbled. "I didn't throw any swings."

"Why not?" Andy asked. "I'd have beat them up in return."

"They were kids."

"You were beat up by kids?" Andy's comment had him straightening in his chair. She quickly changed tactics. "Clearly very dangerous ones."

"I wasn't going to punch a kid," Nathan explained. "Besides," He brushed his fingers over Lina's wrist as her fingers smoothed his hair back from his forehead. "Lina scared them off." He winked at her and a nervous laugh filtered from her lips.

"I don't want to think about that, or the fact my bare foot touched the inside of a subway." She shimmied in disgust and he laughed.

"You were great." He closed his eyes as her fingers continued to lightly flutter over his face checking for injury.

"Lucky for you they weren't good punches," Luke observed.

"For real."

"Tomorrow we'll tap into security footage, get some facial recognition and then charge them for assaulting an officer."

"No." Nathan waved away the suggestion. "It's done."

"Nathan," Lina gently turned his chin towards her. "those boys need to be held responsible. They can't just go around punching people."

"I think they learned their lesson."

"I think me shaking my shoe at them did not teach them anything."

"I think your threat of the authorities scared them enough."

"I disagree." Lina placed her hands on her hips, and he sighed.

"Alright, we'll issue a warning, but that is it." He looked to Luke. "That should scare them enough since it will be coming from the FBI office versus NYPD."

"I guess that will suffice." Lina relaxed. "I'm so sorry. This wouldn't have happened if I hadn't completely messed up the entire evening."

"Oh yeah," Andy interjected. "What was that about anyway? How was your date with Charlie?"

"It was fine." Lina shook away her friend's comment. "And it was just a big misunderstanding."

"I'd say." Andy nodded towards Nathan's face and Lina felt the guilt settle on her shoulders once more.

"I'm so sorry," she whispered, her eyes glassing over as she felt her adrenaline fading and emotion settling in.

Nathan stood to his feet. "I'm fine. I'm glad I was there."

"Could you two give us a minute?" Lina asked Luke and Andy.

"Sure." Luke pointed to the balcony and they stepped outside.

"Nathan—"

"Please do not apologize again," he interrupted, his voice edged with a touch of annoyance. "I've had worse, believe me." She brushed her fingertips over his bruised jaw and he gently clasped her hand. "Seriously, Lina, don't worry over it."

"I feel like I should make it up to you somehow."

His brow quirked. "Oh really?"

Smiling, she sat on the stool next to him. "What would you say to a real dinner? Not a piece of chocolate cake or snacks from the corner market?"

"Hmm..." He rubbed his stubbled chin. "I don't know. I hear comedy clubs are fun."

She playfully punched his shoulder as he laughed.

"Alright, a real dinner. When?"

"Tomorrow."

He pulled a face.

"Is that a no?" she asked.

"I'll be out of town a few days on assignment."

"I'm intrigued, but know I can't ask. How about you just let me know when you're free, and we'll figure something out."

"No. No open-ended invites. Those tend to bleed through the cracks and become forgotten. Let's say next Wednesday. That gives me time to recover from an all-nighter at work. And hopefully for my face to heal up so I'm not such an eyesore."

"You're not an eyesore." Lina defended.

"Well, that's good to know."

She blushed, realizing she'd just complimented his looks.

"Any more blind dates this week?" he asked, and her face sobered.

"I don't even know yet."

"Hey, at least you only have two more."

"*If* I go on them."

"You said tonight wasn't bad."

"But I don't want to see him again. I'm not… looking for that."

"Ah."

"I mean… with him," she amended. His green eyes rested on her face and she fumbled for how to make it sound like it didn't mean she wanted that with *him*, though she found she kind of did. Overall, she surmised that her emotions were out of whack and she couldn't think straight. Which was understandable when Nathan sat there staring at her with the greenest eyes she'd ever seen.

"I should go." His voice interrupted her thoughts as he stood to his feet.

"Right." Lina looked at her watch. "Oh my, it's after ten."

"That it is," Andy's voice called from the doorway and she and Luke stepped back inside. "So you two sort everything out? Lina tell you she has two more blind dates?"

"I'm aware." Nathan smirked as Lina sighed in aggravation.

"Number nine and ten," Andy continued. "And they're good ones. Best for last, you know." She winked at Nathan as if trying to stir him up.

"Oooookay." Lina began nudging Nathan to the door. "She forgets I haven't said yes, yet."

"Oh, yes, you did." Andy reminded her. "Ten dates, remember? *Ten.*" She cackled as Lina all but shoved Nathan out the door and stepped into the hallway with him.

"She really has no shame sometimes."

"She only wants what is best for you, as good friends should."

"Right. Well, I think I can make that decision myself."

"I'm sure you can." He brushed his fingertips over her cheek and her gaze snapped up to his. "I'll be seeing you next Wednesday, Evangelina."

"Wednesday," she confirmed, her heart skipping at the way his eyes danced down to her lips and back up. She took a step towards him. "Take care of yourself, hm? No more fighting teenagers."

He grinned.

She leaned up on her tiptoes and lightly kissed the corner of his mouth that wasn't split. His arm wrapped around her waist, holding her against him as he leaned down to kiss her again.

She placed a hand to his lips, and he stopped with a flush to his cheeks. "We don't want to make that worse." She brushed her thumb over his lip, and he took a deep breath and backed away.

"Stupid busted lip," he muttered.

She smirked. "Maybe it will be better by next Wednesday."

"Oh, I'm going to make sure of it."

She felt the laugh pop out as he smiled on his way to the elevator. He offered one last wave before disappearing into the car.

∞

"She has two more dates, right?" Luke asked. "What are the odds of her finding someone better than you? I mean, she's clearly interested in you, so I doubt she even really tries to connect with the other guys."

"I'm not worried about it."

"Clearly." Luke pointed to the shredded napkin in Nathan's lap as they sat in the cramped sedan, once again watching Peter Gibson enter his office building.

"This guy has yet to do anything suspicious. Other than showing up at the warehouse the other night— which, by the way, is a legitimate flooring business— he hasn't done anything out of the ordinary. Are we sure this is our guy?" Nathan asked.

"So it would seem. The good ones cover their tracks well. And yes, he has acted suspicious. Who goes to a flooring business at three in the morning?"

"There's nothing even traceable to this guy."

"His name came up on a couple of accounts."

"But those accounts have no suspicious activity."

"Their existence is suspicious," Luke countered, his voice edged with a tinge of annoyance.

"I think we're looking in the wrong direction."

"Share that with the SAC then. She's the one that feels Gibson is our ticket."

"Yeah, well, I need more than my gut if I'm going to convince her," Nathan added.

"Definitely." Luke pointed to the napkin pieces. "So, we avoiding that or what?"

"It's nothing." Nathan swiped the remnants off his lap and into an empty coffee cup.

"Andy said she lined a date up for Lina on Friday. That puts her going on a date with you Wednesday and then someone else on Friday. Better make Wednesday a good one if you want to compete."

"I'm not taking her out until *next* Wednesday. So this guy gets the privilege first. You seem to know more about this than I do. Where's the guy taking her?"

"I have no idea. I didn't ask. But she said Lina would like it."

"Great." Nathan's sarcasm had Luke stifling a laugh.

"Hey, look at it this way: if she does, she won't have time for a date number two until after the date with you, so then you can steal the ball back."

"It's not a game," Nathan reminded his friend.

"Sure it is." Luke shrugged his shoulders. "You're trying to win her over, right?"

"I'm trying to get to know her," Nathan corrected.

"Right." Luke rolled his eyes. "Either way, you're trying to be more appealing than the two men she has left on the blind date list. Andy's pumped about the one on Friday. She really thought Lina would like the comedy club guy, but that seemed to fall a little flat."

Nathan liked the sound of that, especially since Lina had already mentioned her feelings to him about that particular date. What could date number nine have planned that is so spectacular, he wondered. His cell phone buzzed, and his Senior Agent in Charge's name lit up the screen. He showed it to Luke before answering.

"Yes ma'am?"

"Pack your bags, Alexander. You're going to DC."

"I'm sorry?"

"I'm pulling you from your current assignment to help with an investigation in DC. They need our best man, and well, you're it. You leave in two hours. Have Howard drop you off at the office. I'll be there with your brief."

He hung up in disappointment.

"What'd she want?"

"We're done here. Take me to the office. I head out for DC in a couple of hours."

Luke whistled under his breath. "Must be big if they're sending you. For how long?"

"No idea. She's going to brief me at the office."

Luke shifted the sedan toward the direction of the field office, the car quiet as they both pondered what type of investigation Nathan would be assisting with. Heading to DC meant it was big, more than likely cyber-attacks on the government's databases. He'd assisted in DC before for that very reason. He hoped that's all it was. Not that it was a good thing, but at least familiar and not altogether time-consuming. Because for once, he didn't want to go anywhere. He wanted to stay in New York and not miss his date with Evangelina Harper. However, next Wednesday, it turned out, just wasn't in the cards.

Chapter Seven

Lina rolled from her printer towards the ringing phone on her desk while attempting to take a swig of coffee before answering. "Evangelina Harper."

"Ms. Harper," Asa's voice rang over the phone. "You have call from a Special Agent Nathan Alexander."

She smirked at his full title, no doubt trying to convince Asa of the urgency of his call since she'd asked him to hold all phone calls for the morning. "Ah, send him through. Thanks, Asa." She waited on the line until a click sounded.

"This is Evangelina." She smiled into the phone as Nathan's voice greeted her.

"Hi, Lina. It's Nathan."

"So I hear, Special Agent Alexander."

He chuckled. "Yeah, about that... he wasn't going to patch me through. I needed to talk with you and I couldn't reach you on your cell."

"That's because it is on silent and I asked him to hold all my calls."

"Busy day then, huh?"

"You could say that." Though she hadn't wanted any interruptions, she wasn't upset at Nathan's call. And just the sounds of his voice had her heart ticking a beat faster.

"Listen, I'm calling because I have to cancel our date next week."

She heard the whoosh of a plane through the receiver as he waited for quiet to return before speaking. "I'm having to go on assignment to DC."

"Oh." She paused in shuffling the papers on her desk to listen. "For how long?"

"That's just it, I don't know. Right now, it's open ended until the investigation comes to a close. Could be a week, a month, or maybe more."

"Oh." This time her voice rang with displeasure.

A heavy sigh told her he wasn't too pleased with the situation either. "Yeah... so I'm a bit annoyed that I'm even having to make this call, but I didn't want to just disappear on you and not give you a reason as to why I might be unreachable for a while."

"I appreciate the call." Lina leaned back in her chair and ran a hand through her hair.

"You're quiet. Did I make a mistake in calling? I really am sorry if I interrupted something important."

"No, no, no, you're fine." Lina leaned forward and rested her elbows on her desk. "I'm just... bummed, I guess, but I totally understand. So I don't want you to think I'm upset with you. I'm just... bummed."

"Me too." Nathan's voice sounded relieved. "I also know you have two more blind dates lined up, which makes me a little more aggravated to be leaving right now."

"I don't think you have anything to worry about there," Lina snickered. "So far, you're the only date that's been a success. Well, and I've just enjoyed our time together outside of the date too. I'm not really looking forward to the last two, but Andy keeps reminding me that I committed to ten of them. And as silly as it sounds, I want to keep my word there, even if I'm kind of dreading them."

"You're being an honorable friend."

"I don't know about that." Lina heard several voices in the background battling for Nathan's attention.

"Well, that's my call," Nathan sighed. "Listen, I know we barely know each other, but I wanted to tell you that I've enjoyed getting to know you. I—"

"Alexander!" a voice called out.

"You should go." Lina could hear the frustration in the other man's tone at having to wait on Nathan.

"Right. Well, I may not be overly reachable for a while. But if I have a chance, I'm going to do my best to reach out to you."

Lina liked the offer but didn't set her hopes too high. "Be safe."

"I will. Take care, Evangelina." He hung up and she slowly placed her phone back into its cradle. Frustration at her own dreary feelings had her dialing Andy's number.

"Hey-o!" Andy greeted with enthusiasm. "I thought you were busy today? Change your mind about lunch?"

"No. I just needed to vent."

"Nathan called you, didn't he?"

"You knew?"

"Luke texted me last night. He said Nathan wanted to be the one to tell you."

"Well, it sucks."

"I'm sorry, Lina. I know you were starting to really like him."

"I was, actually, which is the annoying part. Why can't I fall for the local, boring guy who works on Wall Street and wears a grey suit every day?"

"We tried that. Date number four, remember?"

"How could I forget?" Lina mumbled, thinking of the man who'd kissed her abruptly after scoring a spare in their bowling match. "I guess it's just not my time. Like I told you before all of these dates, I'm just not meant to be with someone right now."

"You don't know that," Andy scolded. "You still have two dates, and you're going to *really* like the next one. I promise."

"So, when should I be hearing from number nine?"

"In a day or so, I imagine. I gave him your number a couple of days ago and he said he was lining things up."

"Sounds intriguing, I guess."

"See, that's the spirit. At the end of this date you'll be saying, 'Nathan, who?'"

Lina smiled into the phone, thankful her friend's optimism cheered her mood. "We'll see. Thanks for the pick-me-up. I needed it."

"That's what I'm here for," Andy reminded her. "Now kick today in the rear and we'll have a girl's night tonight at the apartment. Luke seemed a bit irritated Nathan was reassigned right now too, and he has to work all night because of it. So it looks like I'm a free bird as well."

"Let's order pizza," Lina suggested.

"You read my mind. See you then." Andy hung up and Lina found her mood was slightly lifted at the thought of a comfy night at home.

She hadn't had many of those since she started her blind date spree, so the change of pace would be nice. And she wouldn't have to dress up. She could wear her favorite pair of sweatpants and the oversized t-shirt she'd stolen from her college boyfriend that was still one of her favorites, despite the ending of that relationship years ago. Counting her blessings, she tried to avoid thoughts of Nathan's handsome face, his green eyes, his strong build, and the way her heart skipped when he touched her. If he was to be away for months on end, Lina didn't plan to sit around and wait. She had two more blind dates and then she would get back to her normal way of life. A life she enjoyed, even without a special someone.

Date #9

It was a beautiful day in the city. She'd caught up on her work and Lina felt completely relaxed and ready to take on blind date number nine. She'd dressed in her favorite red blouse with white polka dots, tied her hair back with a red ribbon, and just for fun, painted her lips a deep scarlet to match. If she was to suffer through another date, she was going to do it in style. It'd been a week and she had yet to receive a call or text from Nathan. Clearly, he was busy with work, which she understood, but she was still disappointed. And that just made her want this particular date to at least be fun. She needed something to take her mind off the handsome blond at the crosswalk. Nathan occupied too much of her thought space and she needed a mental break. He was gone, and there was no guessing when he'd be back, *if* he did come back. It was best to just move on. She reached the address and smiled as she realized she'd walked up to a pet shelter. She loved dogs. If she didn't live in a concrete jungle, she'd have bought one years ago. A man, dressed in a navy sweater and jeans stood out front, his hands stuffed in his pockets, shoulders hunched against the cold.

"Timothy?" Lina asked, offering a smile as she walked up.

"Lina?" He extended a hand and she shook it. "Wow, you're beautiful."

She flushed and thanked him for the sweet comment. "So, this is a new one." She pointed to the shelter sign and he grinned.

"I volunteer here each week, so I thought it might be something different."

"It is. I like it."

He opened the door and followed her inside. Pens lined the entry; puppies, kittens, iguanas, and various other small creatures looked up with hopeful eyes. The puppies were adorable, stepping over one another to reach the edge of the pen to yip for attention. But what Lina truly wanted was to see the older animals. The dogs and cats that had been found, dumped, or injured and lost their forever homes. Those were the animals she wanted to love on. Timothy waved her through a door to the right. "I typically work back here."

She saw the pens and the sight broke her heart as the older animals didn't even bother coming to the edge of their pens to greet them. Their gazes were not hopeful, but sad. She counted ten of them. "I want them all."

He smiled. "Yeah, it's pretty sad back here some days. But usually, people don't want the older dogs. They want puppies."

"So what happens to these guys?" Lina asked, squatting in front of a crate housing a pale-yellow Labrador with a gray-tinged face. She stuck her fingers through the slats for him to sniff her and his tail gave two solid thumps at her attention. She tickled under his chin and she could have sworn his eyes sparkled at the loving touch.

"Well, if they don't get adopted out then they will eventually be rotated to another shelter. Though our aim is to adopt them out here, because the shelter they get rotated to is a high kill shelter."

Lina gasped. "No. How awful!" She looked up and saw that Timothy looked on all the animals with compassion and she liked that his heart lined up with hers on that front. "When do they get moved?"

He walked over and pointed to the tag on a pen. "This date is the day they were brought here. This sheet here is their vaccination and care record since being here, and this date," he pointed to the lab's date marked on the bottom of the slip. "is when he'll be shipped out. Looks like this guy leaves in a couple of days."

"Do they have names?"

"Some do. This guy doesn't seem to. Guess whoever dumped him didn't have a collar on him."

"This is so sad." Lina watched as Timothy opened the gate to the lab's crate and tsked his tongue for the older dog to step out and stretch his legs. "What do you do here?"

"I clean the crates, give them fresh water and food, and give them small walks around the room and a little attention."

"And you do this every week?"

Timothy nodded. "Twice a week, every week."

Lina smiled at him as she rubbed a hand over the lab's soft fur. "He'd be adopted right away if people could see him up front."

Timothy shook his head. "They try that during the first couple of weeks after an animal's arrival. After that, they're sort of sifted by age."

"Unbelievable. I don't know how you don't just take them all home." Lina stood and watched as Timothy quickly and efficiently switched out the water bowl and refilled the food bowl in the lab's pen. Lina hooked a leash on the dog's issued collar and began walking him around. "Where all can I take him?"

Timothy pointed to a door. "That leads to a small, fenced-in play area. You can let him loose once he's outside. I'll be out with one of these guys in a minute." He pointed to the next crate over and she walked out into the limited sunshine due to the tall buildings surrounding the shelter.

"Poor thing." She unhooked the dog's leash and watched as he walked around sniffing. He found the one small patch of sunlight on the grass and laid there, rolling over on his back as if relishing the feel of the sun on his fur. "Alright, you're going to make me cry." She walked towards him and rubbed his ears and belly, his feet kicking playfully as she did so. She giggled as he licked her face, and she knew there was no way she could let him stay in a crate and be shipped away in two short days. Andy would kill her if she brought a dog home. Then again, she wouldn't be here if it wasn't for Andy, so really, it was all Andy's fault... or idea... Lina wasn't sure. But she was taking this dog home. There was no question about that.

Timothy stepped out and unhooked the underweight Doberman he'd escorted outside and let him run as Lina studied him. He was tall, a bit lanky, and stylish. He didn't fit what she'd pictured as an animal shelter volunteer, but then again, that was part of his charm. She liked that it was a surprise. He had depth, character, and compassion.

They worked together to walk and play with each of the elderly animals, and when it was time to leave, he walked Lina to the front of the shelter to sign for the Labrador.

"Couldn't help it, hm?" Cheri, the shelter's office manager smirked as she handed Lina a clipboard to sign. She then handed one to Timothy. "Sign and date, Tim. You know the drill. I'll submit your hours in the morning."

Lina's brow furrowed. "Do you volunteer for some sort of organization?"

Cheri harumphed and snatched the clipboard out of Timothy's hands and handed Lina the leash that was clipped to her new dog's collar before walking to the back. Timothy opened the door for her as they walked back onto the city streets.

"No. Community service hours."

Lina's eyes popped as she looked to him again.

He flushed and rubbed a hand behind his neck.

"Court ordered community service?" she asked.

"Yes," he admitted. "Though not for anything serious," he assured her. "Just a little misunderstanding."

"About what?" she asked hesitantly.

"What is considered recreational use and what is prescription use when it comes to certain medicinal products."

"So… drugs?" Lina asked and his avoidance of eye contact told her exactly what she needed to know. Number nine had just scratched himself off the list. Nine down, one more date to go.

Chapter Eight

Nathan snatched his glasses off his face as he entered his hotel room and tossed them onto the overly polished desk that sat void of anything except his laptop and a notebook. The last thing he wanted to do after staring at various screens for the last 48 hours, make that weeks, was look at his own computer. He walked towards the bed and flopped onto his stomach, straight in the middle of the comforter. His cell phone buzzed in his pant pocket and he groaned as he rolled to his back and fished it out. A text from Lina. He sat up quickly, eager to see what she'd sent. A photo appeared of a stunning Lina receiving a sloppy kiss on the cheek from an old dog. "Date Number Nine" she commented underneath and had him laughing. He definitely needed to know the story about date number nine, so he texted her back.

Nathan: *"Best looking date so far."*

Lina: *"Ha! He's pretty handsome."*

Nathan: *"Is he yours?"*

Lina: *"He is now. I'm trying to think of a name. I was thinking Chance. Does he look like a Chance to you?"*

Another picture popped up on the screen of just the dog's sweet face.

Nathan: *"Chance it is."*

He paused a moment and then continued.

Nathan: *"How are you?"*

Lina: *"Good. Been busy at work, but good. And now I'm even better because I get to spoil Chance when I get home."*

Nathan: *"Can't wait to hear the story behind this."*

Lina: *"Any progress on your end?"*

He knew she meant did he know when he'd be finished in DC, but that question required a complex answer, so all he said was: *"Not really."* He hadn't reached out to her for weeks, though he wanted to. He just struggled with leading her on, since he still didn't know when he'd be done in DC. He was being a good guy, right? Or should he have called or texted more? He did say he would, which settled guilt right onto his shoulders.

Lina: *"Well, take care, Nathan."*

He rubbed a palm over his face. *Should he call her? Or should he let it be for now?* He had no clue how long he'd be in DC and felt that wasn't quite fair to both of them to be invested in someone who wasn't around. He decided to call Luke. Luke would know how the date really went and if Nathan should be worried about another man stealing Lina's attention. Because, though he didn't want to lead her on, he also didn't want some other guy swooping in and stealing her attention. His friend answered on the first ring.

"Alexander," Luke greeted. "Miss me yet?"

"Naturally."

Luke chuckled through the phone. "I'm assuming you're calling about the Gibson investigation."

"Right. How's that going?"

"Well, turns out that Brett, the infamous blind date, *is* in league with Gibson after all."

"Oh really? How so?"

"Just one of his many minions. He's talking, though."

"How'd you manage that?" Nathan asked.

"I asked Andy about him a bit more. Said she didn't really know what he did for a living. Then I asked Lina, but she said it never really came up on the date, that he was just a little too distracted by their painting instructor the entire time to really focus on his date with her. And so I did what any good agent would do. I followed him."

Nathan smirked. "And he went to Gibson, or what?"

"No. Turns out Brett is a financial planner. He's clean for the most part other than helping Gibson invest his money. According to Brett, that's the only relationship he has with him. We're running his bank financials now to see if there have been any curious deposits made in the last year or two. But so far, he's clean. So, that's a little bit of a dead end, though we do know Gibson is moving way more money than he should be."

"You'll find something."

Luke sounded tired, but his typical upbeat attitude had him agreeing. "Oh, and Lina asked about you."

"Yeah?"

"She just wanted to check on you. Make sure you were safe."

"She just texted me a picture of her new dog."

"He's a beauty. Old guy, but he's in love with Lina now."

"I look forward to hearing about why she got him."

"And when do you think that will be? How's it going there? Messy case?"

"Complicated is more like it. I can't say much."

"I figured." Luke chuckled. "Well, you better wrap it up, Alexander, if you want a shot with Lina. The woman only has one blind date left, and Andy said after that, Lina has no interest in dating. Basically a 'she tried and nothing worked' sort of mentality."

"If I were there, I'd be pursuing her. No doubt about that."

"But you're not here," Luke reminded him.

"Therein lies the difficulty," Nathan finished. "Probably best for her to find someone else. My work is a bit too unpredictable."

"I'll tell her that."

"What? No."

"Oh, so you don't want her to just move on and find another guy she's interested in?" Luke's grin could be heard through the phone.

Nathan groaned. "I'm still sorting it."

"Sounds like it. I'll let you get back. Call me again if you need updated on the home front."

"Thanks. Later." He hung up feeling marginally better knowing that Lina's ninth date wasn't a successful one. He had assumed, but it was nice to have the confirmation from Luke. What he didn't want was to be gone so long that Lina washed her hands of him and then had zero interest in dating when he returned to New York. But one problem at a time. He lifted his shirt to his nose and cringed. A shower first, then sleep, then a fresh mindset for the next day of computer hacking.

∞

Asa waltzed into Lina's office and clapped his hands. He walked over to her windows and pulled the line to open the blinds and let sunlight in. She squinted at the increased brightness and looked at him. "Asa, what are you doing?"

"Oh, was I not your breath of fresh air?" He motioned towards the door. "I tried to *breeze* in as quickly as possible."

Lina leaned back in her chair and crossed her arms over her chest. "And why did you feel the need to do that?"

"Lina," he began and then corrected himself. "Ms. Harper."

"You can call me Lina, Asa." She added and waved for him to continue.

"Lina, as your assistant, and work friend, I am going to kindly tell you that you have been cranky, sulky, and walking around with a gloomy aura."

Her brows quirked. "Is that so? I had no idea."

"Really?" He pointed to her entirely black wardrobe. "All you've worn this week is black, grey, white, and navy. Where's the vibrant diva I know and love?"

"Diva?" Lina asked amused.

"Yes. What's going on with you? Things not work out with the singing gram guy?"

"Singing gram? Oh, right. No. That didn't work out."

"Really? The flowers were beautiful."

"Two different guys, Asa."

His eyes widened in surprise and a slow smirk spread over his face. "Oh, really?"

She held up her hand. "Not what you think."

"And how do you know what I'm thinking?"

"I see it written on your face." She grinned as she tossed a wadded-up paper at him and he laughed.

"Alright, then tell me what's got you in the grumps."

"I'm not grumpy," she reiterated. "I'm just... busy."

"That is a lie. And I'm offended you would try to pull that one on me."

Sighing, Lina leaned her elbows on her desk and rested her chin on her hands. "It's been a long few weeks, and I'm just tired."

"Okay. Is that all?" Asa asked, still not convinced.

Lina looked to the open door and waved for him to shut it. He hopped out of his seat and quickly closed the door and eagerly plopped back into a chair. "I can tell this is going to be good."

Chuckling, Lina shrugged. "We'll see. I've been going on blind dates."

"Okay…"

"Nine of them."

"*Nine?*"

She nodded. "Yes. Nine. And I'm tired."

"What about the blond man who came into the office with you one day after lunch? Was he one of them?"

"Number seven."

"And that was a bad one?"

"No, actually, he was great. We actually met before our date and didn't realize we'd be seeing one another *on* a date."

"So, he's out of the picture now? I'm confused."

"His work took him out of state, and he doesn't know when he'll be back."

"Ouch."

"Exactly. The other dates have been a no-go, unfortunately."

"And who is setting you up on these dates?" Asa asked.

"My friend, Andy. You've met her."

"Right. I remember her. So, she's scheduling all these dates for you basically?"

"Yes."

"Why?"

Lina took a deep breath. "Because she thinks I work too much and don't date enough. That I'm just wasting away in my office." She smirked at his nod of agreement. "So I agreed to go on ten dates."

"Ten? That means you have one more."

"Yep."

"When is it?"

"Next Friday."

"With who?"

"I have no idea."

Asa tapped his chin. "So, you have another date, but you sort of have feelings for number seven?

But he's pulled out of the equation because of work, and so now you're all bummed out?"

"I wouldn't say I have feelings for him. And can we please call him Nathan. I feel horrible calling him just Number Seven."

"Okay, so Nathan is MIA and you're wishing he wasn't?"

Her discomfort at sharing her feelings with Asa was written on her face and he rolled his eyes. "Just admit it, Lina."

"Okay. Yes. I liked him. I even considered pursuing more dates with him. But now he's gone without a clue as to when he'll be back. And I have one blind date left, and I'm tired of dating. Like, over it. But then part of me wonders if it could be a guy like Nathan. That maybe number ten will be a fantastic guy and I'll be missing out. But then I kick myself because I like my life the way it is. Is it really that bad to want to be single? And then Andy tells me I just feel that way because I haven't met someone special. And then my mind goes back to Nathan, which then confuses me again because he's gone now, you know? It's not like I can pursue him even if I wanted to. So overall, I'm just confused and tired and frustrated with the whole thing. And though I want to be hopeful of the last date, I'm secretly dreading it. Because if I like this guy, and Nathan does come back soon, then I'm tied up with someone else. It's just easier to be by myself. And with my new dog," she added quickly at the end.

Asa leaned back in his chair as if he'd been slammed with too many facts at one time.

"Aren't you glad you asked?" Lina laughed.

Asa rested an arm on the arm rest and leaned his chin on his fist as her words whirled in his head. "Do you want my advice?"

"Sure. Why not?"

"Go on date number ten. See how it goes. If you don't go, you'll wonder. And if you do go and have a great time, great. If you go and it's another miss, fine. You'll have tried."

"But what about Nathan?"

"What about him?" Asa asked. "He's gone. Have you been keeping in touch?"

"A little."

"How much is a little? Like you two talk for hours on end or just a few texts here and there?"

"Just a few texts. So far."

"Then go on date number ten. As of right now, Nathan is just a slight blip on the radar. If he wanted to be more than that, he'd be blowing up your phone all the time over the smallest things. Trust me, I know. I'm a guy. If I'm interested in someone, they know."

"But—"

"No buts, Lina. If he's interested, he'll step up his game, even if he is long distance."

"Alright." She exhaled a deep breath. "You're right. I need to just move on from our time together and focus on whatever lies ahead."

"Exactly."

"This has actually been quite refreshing, Asa. Thank you."

"You're welcome." He smiled. "It helps sometimes to talk it out with someone who is impartial."

"You're right. It kind of does."

"However," he continued. "Now you have to tell me about all the dates up to this point." A wicked gleam sparkled in his eyes as he relaxed further back into her chair and crossed his arms, as if resolute and not leaving until she complied. Lina's lips twitched. "Linda's going to be upset with you," she told him as she pressed the intercom button on her phone to contact one of the secretaries at the front of the office. "Linda, will you please hold my calls. Asa and I will be working in my office. And could you please send two lattes up. Thanks." She released the button and looked to her assistant. "If we're going to talk, then we're going to work on organizing these." She grabbed a stack of manuscripts from behind her desk that had been mixed and unorganized. "Sort by title and page number," she ordered. "In the time I tell you about all of these dates, we should have my entire office organized."

Asa rubbed his hands together before hopping to his feet and walking to a small closet in Lina's office and removing a fold-out table. He popped the legs and unfolded the table, setting it up in front of her windows as he began sifting and separating the piles of pages she had given him. Lina moved from behind her desk and pulled a large cardboard box towards the table.

"What is that?" Asa asked.

"More pages."

He took a step back and grunted. "We need to work on your organizing system, Lina. Big time."

"They're scanned into my computer in perfectly neat files."

"Right, well, this is ridiculous."

"Oh, would you rather me have Linda in here helping? You could answer my calls, sift through emails, and—"

"Nope. No, I'm good," Asa laughed. "Now, get to talking."

Chapter Nine

Date # 10

It didn't take Lina long to reach East Village. In fact, she actually made the trek across the city rather quickly. The metro, thankfully, popped her out just two blocks from the waterfront restaurant where she'd be meeting blind date number ten in less than a half hour. He'd chosen a restaurant on the East River; she'd give him points there. The city lit up at night was a beautiful sight. Andy assured her the location was "all his idea" and that she merely suggested Italian food, knowing it was Lina's favorite. Either way, Lina wasn't disappointed in the choice, especially since it wasn't a fancy place. She wasn't in the mood to wear a cocktail dress for the evening. Instead, she opted for a cute pair of black skinny jeans, an emerald green blouse, and black heels, topped with her favorite pea coat for warmth. She walked up to the restaurant and opened the door to the smell of garlic and herbs, her mouth watering at the thought of fresh bread dipped in olive oil and balsamic.

"Lina?"

A smooth, deep voice to her left had her turning to find a tall man dressed in jeans and a fitted charcoal sweater. He gave a nervous smile that quickly flashed a dazzling set of dimples and perfectly straight teeth. "Hi."

He extended his hand. "I'm Callen."

She shook his hand. "Nice to meet you. Great choice, by the way." She circled her hand to encompass the room.

"One of my favorites. I have us a table outside, if that's alright?"

"Of course."

"They have heaters set up and it's not too cold. But if you do get chilly, please let me know."

"I'm sure it's great." She smiled and was pleased when he guided her towards their table with a hand at the small of her back. He pulled out her chair and waited for her to sit before he claimed his own seat across from her. So far, so good. He had manners. He was good looking. He seemed a little nervous, as was she. And he had good taste in food.

"Andy tells me you're an editor at Armm and Goode Publishing."

"That's right."

"Have you been there long?"

"About six years." Lina looked up as the waiter placed a basket of warm rolls and a small plate with oil and vinegar in front of them and hurried off.

"I pass your building on Wednesdays and Fridays. I've seen the sign on the listing, but I've never ventured inside. There's a lot of different businesses in that building."

"Yes. We're on the twenty-third floor. I think there's another publishing house a few floors below us, but I couldn't tell you the name. I'm sort of in my own little bubble when I'm there."

"Well, you obviously like your bubble if you've been there for so long." He smiled as he unrolled his napkin and utensils and placed his napkin in his lap.

"I do. It's great. I love what I do. I'm sort of a nerd when it comes to grammar, and I love seeing stories in their rawest form and seeing them take shape into what you find on the bookshelves. It's a neat process."

"Sounds like it. I love books. I have way too many."

She perked up at this news and leaned forward. "Really? What do you enjoy reading?"

He tilted his head back and forth as if trying to come up with a sensible answer. "Anything." He laughed. "I mean, I like all genres and I like non-fiction. Just depends on what I'm in the mood for. Currently I'm reading a thriller by Vincent Grady that's part of a rather large series. I think I am on book nine."

She smiled. "Vincent is one of our authors at Armm and Goode."

"Really?"

"Yes, though I don't edit his books. I'm mostly historical fiction. But Lou, two offices over, is usually his editor."

Callen waved for her to help herself to the rolls.

She reached forward and placed one on a small plate in front of her. "I hope you don't think I'm unladylike, but I am starving." She tore a piece off the roll and dipped it in the oil.

"Hey, I'm the one that was offering for you to take one because I didn't want to be rude and grab one before you."

"No judgement here." Lina raised her hands as she smiled. So far, she liked Callen. He seemed genuine and laid back and completely open to learning about her and not just talking about himself. "And what do you do for a living?"

He grimaced and Lina felt her stomach drop with the familiar preparation for disappointment. But instead, he said, "I'm an accountant."

Her stomach muscles loosened, and she grinned. "What's wrong with that?"

"It sounds dreadfully boring compared to what you do."

"Boring? I edit grammar for a living." She laughed. "Most people would find that boring."

"I crunch numbers."

"I crunch words."

He lifted his glass of water. "Well, then here's to our crunching careers then."

Smiling, she clinked her glass to his. "To crunching."

Lina listened as he talked more about his time in New York and where he grew up. She liked that the conversation flowed easily and that he was equally interested in her past and family. She'd yet to talk to any of the men about her family, even Nathan, but Callen was warm. He radiated so much positive energy and likability that she started warming up to the idea that she might just want to see him again after this initial date. Maybe Andy was right, she'd saved the best for last.

Her alfredo pasta was divine, and she had zero problem eating every last bite of it, as Callen did the same to his. Overall, the date was a breath of fresh air and she found she didn't quite want it to end yet. That was new. She looked up as the waiter cleared their dishes. "If you'll excuse me a minute, I'm going to visit the ladies' room before we head out."

"Go right ahead." He reached for his glass and just looked out over the river as she walked towards the restroom. She grabbed her phone out of her pocket and saw various messages from Andy asking how it was going. She sent a quick reply of a thumbs up and focused on her reflection in the mirror. She did the ridiculous motions of a woman on a date by fluffing her hair, checking her eyeshadow and mascara, reapplying her lipstick, and even giving herself a small squirt of her perfume as she prepared for at least a few more minutes of Callen's company. Her phone buzzed as she was about to walk out, and she saw Nathan's name pop up on the screen of her cell phone. She hesitated a moment. *Should she even look at it while she was out with Callen?* She was having a great time with her date, would engaging with Nathan alter that? She still liked him, but she'd just started growing comfortable with the possibility that maybe there was another option here in New York. Was there any point in pursuing Nathan when he wasn't here?

She decided to ignore the text until she got home. She wanted to be fair to Callen. She stuffed her phone in her purse and headed back to the table. Callen stood and motioned towards the river. "Would you be up for a walk in the park along the water?"

She nodded. "I'd like that." He extended his hand and she clasped it as he wound their way through the restaurant and out the door. He didn't release it when they stepped outside until he helped her into her jacket. "Dinner was amazing. Thank you."

"You're welcome." He smiled down at her as they turned towards the sidewalk that would lead them down into the park.

Lina had never walked along the East River. She only ventured to the area for food here and there and stayed mostly close to Manhattan. But the park was lit with streetlamps and they weren't the only couple enjoying the city's reflection on the water. They wound their way through the quiet and towards the water's edge, reaching a private corner with a bench overlooking the water. Callen motioned towards it and Lina thought it perfect to continue their conversation from the restaurant. But before she could sit, a man, dressed in an oversized coat, worn shoes, and torn pants, popped out of the shadows. She jumped and placed a hand to her heart as he hissed at them. He reached into his coat pocket and pulled out a small blade and brandished it towards them. Lina went to step back and reach for Callen, but he wasn't there. She quickly turned her head and he'd taken cautious steps backwards, his hands in surrender as he eyed the man curiously. She turned back to the bum and avoided his hand as he reached for her. Demanding money, the man pointed his box cutter at her bag. She shook her head and began to back away slowly, hoping to reach Callen before the man decided to make more of an attempt. He was definitely experiencing a high on some sort of drug because he couldn't focus, his words were jumbled, and his motions were unpredictable. Lina knew, though, that despite that, his adrenaline was probably pumping, and he'd be stronger than he looked.

"Callen," she nervously called over her shoulder.

"Just give him what he wants, Lina." Callen's voice rang with nerves and she stood appalled that he continued his retreat, leaving her to fend for herself. A lightbulb flickered on in her head as she reached into her purse and clasped her only hope.

The man took a step towards her, swiping his blade and arm towards her elbow as if to grab her and pull her towards him. Pulling her hand out of her purse, she brandished her own means of protection and pressed the button. The taser connected, and the drugged bum crumbled to his knees, screaming in agony before he fell to the ground and twitched. Breathless, Lina collected herself and ran, ignoring Callen, and mentally marking him off the list. Date number ten was done.

∞

"You *tased* him?" Andy's alarm had her rushing towards Lina and enveloping her in her arms. She pulled back and rubbed her hands up and down Lina to instill some warmth. Luke stood in the kitchen, the cookie he held halfway to his mouth completely forgotten as he stared in shock.

Lina rubbed a hand through her hair. "I just ran. I mean, what else was I supposed to do? Callen just backed away and stood there. I don't even know where he is now. I just took off and didn't stop running until I hopped into the subway car." She held a hand over her rapidly beating heart. "I'm okay, right?" She looked to Luke. "I mean, I won't go to jail?"

This seemed to bring him back down to earth as he tossed his cookie on the counter and walked towards her. He drew her into his arms and Lina, despite not knowing Luke well, sank into the comfort and strength he offered. "No jail for you, Wonder Woman. You did great. Smart thinking. And I'm happy to hear you have something with you for protection." He rubbed her back, his eyes connecting with Andy over the top of Lina's head, both realizing how dangerous the night had been for her.

She pulled away. "Thanks. I didn't know what to do; if I should call in the situation to the police or just let it be."

"Let it be," Luke told her, his gruff order telling the women he was going to see to it that the bum was taken care of somehow.

Lina blew a relieved breath and sank onto a stool, the adrenaline and flight leaving her system. "So that was date number ten."

Andy flashed a sympathetic smile. "Sorry, I really thought you two would hit it off."

"Oh, we did. Callen was great. I actually found myself looking forward to a second date. But not after that creepy guy hopped out and threatened to cut me with a box cutter and Callen just fed me to the wolves."

"Yeah, I don't think I'd pursue that guy," Luke suggested, quieting when Andy flashed him a frustrated glance.

"Yeah." Lina sighed. "Bummer. But you know, it's all okay. I can get back to normal and—" She hopped to her feet, frantic, as she realized her new dog hadn't greeted her at the door which was his custom. "Where's Chance?"

"Don't worry." Luke pointed to an oversized floor cushion that was nestled in the living room against the wall. "He's enjoying his new bed."

"Where did that come from?" Lina asked.

Andy pointed to Luke. "He brought it."

"You bought my dog a bed?"

"Sorry if I overstepped. Met him the other day. Love him, by the way. He just looked up at me and asked me to buy him a bed."

"Oh, he asked you?" Lina grinned.

"With those soulful brown eyes of his. It was like, I didn't realize what I was doing until I was trying to ride the subway with this giant dog bed."

Lina and Andy laughed.

"Well, thank you. He obviously loves it."

"Hasn't moved much since Luke put it down," Andy said.

Lina walked over to Chance. "Hey, buddy." The dog's tail thumped when he spotted her, and he raised to a sitting position to lick her cheek and excitedly welcome her home. He then made an excited circle to show off his new comfortable spot. Lina scratched him behind the ears and let him settle back onto his stomach as she walked back to her friends. "He seems perfectly content."

"So, I texted you like a thousand times tonight."

"I know. I'm sorry. I was having a good time, so I didn't want to be rude. Oh, that reminds me..." She fished her phone out of her purse. "Nathan texted me earlier and I didn't respond to him either."

Andy and Luke shared another glance.

"Guess I can now." Lina started to type into her phone and then set it on the counter. "You know what? No. I'm not going to. Not right now."

"Why not?" Andy asked. "You've liked Nathan since you met him at the coffee shop."

"And he's not even in New York."

"So? He'll be back. Eventually," Andy added.

Lina looked to Luke and he inhaled a deep breath as if unsure what she wanted to hear from him. "I don't have much to offer you there, Lina. I mean, sometimes these investigations take months. And Nathan's one of the best, so they'll keep him there to see it through. However, I also know he's a great guy, who happens to think you've hung the moon. So, it's up to you. I don't think he'd blame you, though, if you backed off. He knows the hurdles his work brings to any relationship or friendship. I mean, I guess we all do, really. Agents, I mean. Not many people can live with what we do or our crazy schedules. It's one of the hazards of the job." Andy reached towards his hand and clasped it, showing her support of his work in a quiet, yet meaningful way.

Lina eyed her phone, contemplating her next move. "His work doesn't bother me," she said. "If anything, tonight makes me appreciate it more because I know if I were with Nathan, he'd have stood his ground and helped me." She reached for her phone and opened the text message, her eyes popping up to Luke's. "Have you talked with him today?"

His brow furrowed. "No. Why?"

She turned her phone towards him so he could read Nathan's hopeful text of wrapping up his investigation in a matter of days. Luke's lips twitched. "See, I knew Alexander wouldn't stay away too long." He winked at her and she felt a flush hit her cheeks.

"I guess you'll be responding to his message now, then." Andy wriggled her eyebrows as Lina waved away her teasing.

"Maybe. I still haven't decided." Lina playfully stuck out her tongue. "But first, I feel like I've battled giants tonight. I'm going to take a hot bath, relax, and then maybe I'll respond to Nathan."

"You better. Or I'm going to set you up on another date," Andy warned her.

Lina waved a hand over her shoulder on her way to her room. "Good night." Her tone playful, but final, as she brushed a quick hand over Chance before slipping into her room.

Chapter Ten

A few days turned to weeks. But thankfully, weeks did not turn into months before Nathan stepped into his office in New York and found Luke tapping away on his computer. Luke glanced up and did a double take as he watched Nathan place a duffle bag into his desk chair across from him. "Well, hey partner. Welcome back."

"Thanks."

"And all is well in DC?"

"For now." Nathan smirked, rubbing a hand over his tired face.

"And when did you get into town?"

"Just now."

"You been home yet?"

"No."

"Why not?" Luke asked.

"SAC wants to brief me on everything that's happened here in my absence."

"I could have done that." Luke rolled his eyes as he nodded towards the SAC's office behind Nathan. "Better get to it. She's been on a war path this morning."

Nathan ran a hand through his hair and walked towards his superior's office door and knocked. He entered at her greeting and closed the door behind him.

"You look terrible, Alexander."

"Thanks. It was a long night. Red eye flights don't agree with me like they used to."

"Well, I appreciate you coming in straightaway. I've another assignment for you, should you want it."

His brow quirked as he listened to her discuss a current investigation needing his expertise. There were other people as qualified as he was, other agents that could head off whenever needed, but the request had come for him. He sighed and she paused. "I take that reaction as a sign you're not really interested."

"No ma'am, I'm not."

"You do realize that there's a chance this could—" He held up his hand to pause her explanation.

"I realize every hazard, complication, opportunity, etc."

Her face softened as she sat behind her desk. "But you're still wanting to stay grounded for a bit?"

"Exactly. I am mentally fried. I've currently been awake for almost thirty-six hours."

"Then that settles it. I'll let the Los Angeles office know they will need to dip into the Baltimore office on this one."

"Thanks."

"You will need to partner with Howard on the status of his investigation into Gibson. Pick up where you left off there. His status report last week had some new findings."

"Yes ma'am."

"But first, Nathan, go home. Get some rest. Come back tomorrow." He stood, nodding his understanding as he walked back towards his desk.

"Well?" Luke asked.

"Dodged having to turn around and go to Los Angeles."

"Nice."

"Yeah. I'm going to head out and be back tomorrow, after some sleep."

"I figured you'd be on the way to Lina's office." Luke glanced up and sat in surprise at Nathan's curious expression.

"Why would I do that?"

"Well, you two have been keeping in touch, right?"

"Not for a few weeks."

Baffled, Luke straightened in his chair. "What? What happened?"

Nathan shrugged his shoulders. "Guess she got tired of waiting for me to come back. I don't blame her. I texted her prematurely about being back in a few days, and that turned into weeks. Not exactly a great start to building trust in what I say. And she never even responded to that message anyway, so I just assumed she's moved on."

"Wait." Luke stood to his feet. "You mean to tell me Lina never texted you back that night?"

"What night?"

"Of her tenth blind date?"

Nathan shook his head. "I guess not. I didn't realize she'd already had it."

Luke chuckled. "Oh man, yeah she did. I figured you'd be the first person she'd tell. In fact, I thought she'd planned to. We literally talked and teased her about texting you that night."

"Guess she changed her mind."

"Andy is going to be livid."

Nathan held up his hand. "Look, I don't want to push her, alright. She's made up her mind. I don't want to bombard her with guilt or sympathy or whatever. She isn't interested anymore. I get it." Worn out and somewhat disappointed, Nathan gave a tired smile. "Now leave me alone. I'm going home. I'm going to sleep. I'll see you tomorrow."

Luke shook his hand. "Fair enough. Later."

Nathan shouldered his duffle bag and headed for the elevator. He waved at Thames on his way out, the smell of hot dogs teasing him towards his favorite street vendor at the end of the block. He hadn't eaten in over twelve hours, and though the line was long, he knew it'd be worth the wait to fill his stomach before hibernating the next twelve hours. His stomached growled as he watched person after person turn from the cart with their indulgent feast and walk away. He was now five people away from his own blissful meal when the woman at the front turned, her hands full with two hot dogs, her purse hanging on the crook of her elbow. Lina. She didn't see him, her attention focused on not losing one of her hot dogs as she attempted to adjust her heavy purse to a more comfortable position. She walked towards him, pausing to readjust an arm's length away. Torn, he wasn't sure whether to say anything, but then it looked as if she were about to lose one of her hot dogs, so he stepped over and grasped her hand in his. Her eyes darted up at the assistance and she gasped as her hold relinquished completely and he fumbled catching her food. She jolted, her hands nervously stabilizing the paper trays as well as she came to terms with his presence. When they'd righted her trays, and her purse sat snuggly on her shoulder, her eyes found his. "Nathan."

"Hi, Lina." He smiled.

"Wh- How— when—" She paused and then let out a nervous laugh. "Wow, I'm just surprised. When did you get back?"

He glanced at his watch. "About an hour ago."

"Really?" Her eyes widened and then they roamed over his face, his clothes, his bag. "It's good to see you." She looked around and scurried to place her paper trays on a free patio table on the sidewalk. She then rushed back over to him to continue their conversation.

"Hey, don't let them grow cold on my account." He nodded towards her food.

"Oh, well, it's fine. I—"

"Lina," He smiled at her. "you have a few minutes?"

"Well, yes. I'm on my lunch break."

"Then give me a few minutes." He reached for her hand and squeezed it. "I'll grab some food and meet you at the table, if you want?"

"Of course." She smiled, her eyes watchful as he took another step forward in line. She moved with him as if he might disappear at any moment. He liked that she wanted to see him, or seemed to, anyway. He looked down at her and she flushed. "Right. I'll just… wait over there." Her heels clicked as she rushed to her table and sat; her hands, he noticed, fumbling with nerves as she unwound her napkin. She hadn't expected to see him, and who could blame her, but the fact his presence made her nervous was an interesting find. Perhaps surprising her in this way was best. Her reaction was genuinely pleased despite her shock. And that encouraged him greatly.

He ordered his food and walked towards the table, only Lina was gone. Her food was there, but the woman had vanished. He paused, glancing around. It was then he saw her rushing back towards the table carrying two bottles of water she'd purchased from another vendor. She met him at the table with a welcoming smile and placed one in front of him.

"Thanks."

"You're welcome." She slid into her chair, her legs bouncing underneath with nervous energy as she watched his every move.

"I'm really here," he told her.

She blinked then, realizing she'd been staring. "Sorry, I'm being rude."

"No," he chuckled. "I get it. It's been a while."

"Yeah, it has. How are you?"

"Tired." His honest reply made her eyes soften as she reached a hand towards his arm and then hesitated before dropping it back to her lap, as though questioning whether or not her touch would be welcome. "But good," he added. "You?"

"Oh, same old, same old." She grinned. "Just work these days."

"No more dates?" he asked.

Her cheeks turned crimson. "No. Thankfully. Number ten is done and my life is back to normal."

"I'm sorry to hear that."

She looked perplexed.

"I mean, sorry number ten didn't work out."

"Oh," She brushed his comment away. "I'm not. It was... well, let's just say it followed the pattern of most of the other ones. But that was weeks ago, so no use thinking about midnight muggings and box cutters, right?"

"Whoa, what?" He stiffened in his chair. "Mugging? Were you mugged?"

Her brows lifted. "Oh, I assumed Luke had told you."

He shook his head. "No. Are you okay? Where was this? *When* was this?"

She placed a calming hand on his arm and the touch had them both snapping to attention at the spark that was still there. A heavy silence hung in the air between them, their eyes focused sharply on one another as conversation stopped. Nathan waited, though he wished to jump out of his skin at her touch. He wanted to scoop her in his arms and kiss her senseless, but that was over the top, wasn't it? They hadn't spoken in weeks, and on top of that, they still didn't know each other super well. But something about Lina had him battling emotions he'd never faced before. "Nathan," Her voice was quiet as her eyes searched his. She cleared her throat and broke eye contact. "We should eat. My disastrous dates shouldn't be the only topic of conversation." She fidgeted as she tucked her hair behind her ears. "Tell me about DC. Well, what you can anyway."

And just like that, the moment was gone, and though he was disappointed to see her avoid the chemistry in the air, he understood it wasn't the time or place to explore it. Encouraged that the hum between them was indeed still there, he was relieved and determined, but he'd give her laidback chatter and conversation this go round. Time would come for them to sort out what was brewing between them. At least, that's what he hoped. He filled her in on what details of his work he could, which was limited and cryptic. He hated he couldn't be completely open with her about such things.

She glanced at her watch and regretfully gathered her trash. "I have to be getting back to the office. It was fun bumping into you. I'm glad you're back and in one piece it seems." She smiled. "You look completely exhausted, but I thank you for taking time to eat with me."

They walked their trash to the bin, and he fell into step beside her towards her office. "I'm glad I did too. I'm sorry I didn't message you that I was headed back. It's just last time I did, the time frame changed, and I didn't want that to happen again."

"I'm sorry I didn't respond." She looked up sheepishly. "That night was bit crazy, and I just needed some space from everything and everyone."

Still not knowing what exactly happened on her tenth date, Nathan responded in kind. "I understand. Sometimes we need that breather."

Reaching her office building, he held back as she paused by the revolving doors. "Listen," she took a step back towards him. "once you're rested and caught up with... getting back into the swing of things, I wouldn't mind having lunch with you again. If you're up for it."

His heart tugged and he felt instant relief flood through him. "Yes. I'd definitely be up for that. And I'm happy to hear you say you would be too."

"Well, I have to have someone to eat greasy hot dogs with, right?" Lina smiled, her upbeat temperament back in place.

"Exactly. Not many are willing to damage their arteries these days."

She laughed and then softly nibbled on her bottom lip as she studied him again. Someone stepped between them to walk into the building, and she cleared her throat. "Right, well, I'm headed back to work. You have a lovely rest, Nathan, and I will look forward to hearing from you before spring."

"If I hibernate that long, send help."

She grinned as she waved and walked inside, pausing briefly to flash her smile once more through the window before heading towards the elevator. Content, Nathan found his steps lighter as he navigated his way towards home and what would be a blissful, long nap.

∞

Lina snatched the bag of cheddar popcorn from Andy's grasp and tucked herself into the corner of the couch, one leg hanging to the floor to bury itself in Chance's fur. He took every toe tickle he could as he breathed steadily beneath her.

"All I'm saying, is that you could have invited him over tonight," Andy said, reaching for her glass of soda. Luke rummaged in the refrigerator, his constant presence at their apartment during his free time becoming more and more of a norm. Lina didn't mind. She could tell Andy liked him and was borderline falling in love with the man already. Luke, though she could tell he was trying to maintain somewhat of a distance with Andy, was clearly tangled up over her roommate just as much. But Lina figured he'd yet to admit that to himself. He raised his head and sighed. "I can't find the salsa."

"Oh, check the cabinet," Lina yelled. "I bought a new jar the other day."

He snapped his fingers as he walked towards the far cabinets and began his search over there.

"And to answer you," Lina turned her attention back to Andy. "He looked exhausted. He needed to recuperate, and quite frankly seeing him again had me... I don't know, all mushy inside." She rubbed her heart. "Like, all I wanted to do was kiss him.

And that's ridiculous. I haven't seen him in over a month, we've barely spoken the last few weeks, and I'm just not sure I want to feel mushy right now."

"Mushy? Is that a technical term?" Luke gave her a quick wink as he found a seat by Andy on the couch with his jar of salsa and bag of tortilla chips.

"I'm sorry, Luke. I know you and Nathan are close and here I am telling you things that I probably shouldn't."

"I don't mind. I like this whole game you guys are setting in motion."

"Game? I'm not trying to play games." Lina, offended, halted in her movement of taking a sip of her drink.

"I didn't say you were playing games. I said you were preparing to. But not a bad game. You and Alexander are just going to sidestep one another for a while. He's all 'I think she's incredible, but don't want to come on too strong' and you're all 'he makes me feel all mushy, but I don't want to date right now'. It's going to be fun to watch."

Lina and Andy's narrowed gazes had him pausing as he held a chip to his lips. "What?"

Andy rolled her eyes at him as Lina smirked. "Your honesty is refreshing, Luke. But I don't like it." She bit back a smile as he laughed and shrugged.

"Nathan thinks I'm incredible, huh?"

Luke's face blanched as he realized he'd shared his friend's feelings without first talking to him. "Well... of... I guess," he added, avoiding eye contact. "I probably shouldn't have told you that. But since I'm not in the fifth grade, I'm going to just tell you that he's still interested and hoping that his absence hasn't totally screwed up his chances at getting to know you better. And that's all I'm going to say, because he should be the one to tell you that in person."

Lina snuggled deeper into the couch and found herself distracted as the movie Andy'd picked started its opening credits. Nathan was interested in her. Despite her other dates, despite being gone, and despite the awkwardness earlier in the day, he was still interested. She reached for her phone. A harmless text to check in on him was okay, wasn't it? And *if* he happened to be rested maybe he could join them? No. She set her phone down. No, she wasn't going to do that. She wanted time to herself, didn't she? But the way Nathan's green eyes caressed her face at lunch had her stomach clenching. "Luke?" Lina interrupted the movie and Andy groaned, pausing the picture on the screen with a playful smirk. "I need a favor."

"Name it." Luke looked over and a slow smile spread on his face. "Where do you want him to meet you?"

"Mode. Seven." Lina hopped to her feet and ran to her room to dress.

"Got it." Luke pulled out his cell phone and dialed Nathan's number. A second later, a groggy response could be heard through the receiver. "Hey man, you get some rest?" Luke asked.

"A bit. What's up?"

"Feel like a blind date tonight?"

"Not really."

"Come on, I know you'll like her. Besides, I figured you'd need someone to get your mind off of Lina for a bit."

"Who said I needed to do that?"

"Me. And Andy. She agrees."

"I haven't even seen Andy since I've been back," Nathan mumbled.

"Look, she has this friend... super cute, nice, and fun. I think you'll like her," Luke continued.

"And what about Lina? Andy doesn't think I should hold out hope there, huh?" Nathan asked.

"No. We think you should move on." Luke grinned at Andy as she shook her head and bit back a smile.

A heavy sigh later, Nathan asked. "What time?"

"Ha! I knew you'd be game. Seven at Mode."

"Mode, again? Really? The place I actually went on a date with Lina? Don't you think that's a little too weird?"

"What? It's a good place and I know I can get a reservation set up."

"Fine. But this girl better be worth it, because I'm still tired. And frankly, I'm a little disappointed. After seeing Lina today, I felt... hopeful. Guess I misread her."

"Sounds like it. Alright, seven. Don't be late." Luke hung up and looked to Andy. "I'm a terrible friend."

"No, you're not. You're giving him a surprise."

"For what though?"

They both glanced up as Lina stepped out of her room, dressed in a pearl-colored cocktail dress and stilettos. Luke gave a low whistle. She looked up. "Okay, how do I look?" She did a spin and smiled at Andy's thumbs up.

"And what do you have planned for Nathan exactly?" Andy asked.

"Well, I'm still working that out," Lina admitted. "But I *do* know I'd be stupid to pass up the feelings he's stirred inside me. I mean, just seeing him today made me want to just slide into his arms and soak him up." She pointed a finger at Luke. "Don't laugh."

"I wasn't." He leaned back and crossed his arms over his chest and one ankle over the other with a satisfied smile.

"We connected before he left, and there was this moment at lunch today that I felt like that connection was about to burst. In a good way. And that feeling wouldn't be there if I weren't interested or if he weren't interested. Which," She waved her hand at Luke, "you say he might be. So, I'm going to give it a shot."

"Oh really?" Andy asked, excited and now standing and helping Lina into her jacket.

"Yes." Lina spun around and gave Andy a hug. "I'll let you know how it goes." She was out the door like a whirlwind leaving only her signature fragrance behind.

Chapter Eleven

Nathan sat at the bar and sipped on a glass of wine, checked his watch, and noted his date was just a few minutes late. He'd told the hostess to come find him when the other half of his party arrived, but he'd yet to be tapped on the shoulder. A woman, looking to be about twenty years his senior, sat next to him, her small sequin purse resting on the bar top. She gave him an appreciative glance before ordering her own wine. Red painted nails inched their way towards his arm, and he knew she was about to engage him in conversation. He wasn't in the mood. He was only here because Luke and Andy seemed to think their friend would be a nice woman for him to get to know. Though he'd admit he was a bit bitter they didn't seem to think he could redeem himself with Lina, he'd shown up at Mode anyway.

The hand found his forearm and she inched closer, leaning in to reveal more than he'd hoped to see when he turned to face her. Her lips were painted as red as her nails and they spread over exceptionally white teeth that told him she'd paid a pretty penny to keep them so. As she started to open her mouth, Nathan felt his opposite shoulder being tugged, and his stool spun around to a smiling Lina. "Hey, you! Fancy meeting you here!" She plopped on the stool to his left and the older woman slinked away with a pout. "Did I interrupt something?"

He stared at her, his mouth agape a moment as he shook his head. "Lina." His eyes darted around, nervous that his new date would now show up when Lina was sitting next to him. He didn't want her to think he was... what? That he was on the market for someone else? "Hi. What are you doing here?"

"Well," She leaned towards him, a gleam in her eye. "I am on date number eleven, actually."

He glanced towards the front of the restaurant. "I thought you only committed to ten. He's not here yet, I'm guessing?"

"Not sure. Mind if I sit with you for a bit?"

"Not at all." He motioned for the bartender and ordered her a white wine, remembering that to be her drink of choice the last time they were here.

"So, what brings you here? Got a hot date as well?"

"Something like that, I guess. Luke called me. He and Andy had it in their heads to send me on another blind date too. Why do we let them?" he asked on a clipped laugh.

"Because we love them," Lina said, and thanked the bartender for the fresh glass. "So what time are you meeting your date?" she asked.

"Supposed to be seven." He nodded towards his watch. "That was ten minutes ago, so I'm not feeling hopeful. You?"

Her quiet response had him tilting his head to look at her and it was then he saw her grin. "Wait... are you my date?"

She nodded. "Yes. Hope you don't mind."

His shoulders relaxed and he reached for her hand, which she gladly let him take. "You have no idea how much I do not mind."

She giggled nervously as he brushed his thumb over her knuckles. "I asked Luke to call you."

His brows rose as she began motioning her hands as she spoke. "I know it sounds crazy, but I was sitting there tonight, thinking about our lunch together and just... you. And I thought, I want to see him. I know you've been gone for a while and we didn't quite have much of a foundation when you left, but I'd like to remedy that. Lunch showed me today that I... well, I still wanted to get to know you."

"Lina—"

"So, hi. My name's Lina. I like coffee dates, chocolate cake, flowers, riding on subways with federal agents while avoiding teenage ruffians, and men who wear glasses."

Nathan bit back a laugh. "Well, it's nice to meet you, Lina. My name's Number Seven." She giggled as he continued. "And I like... you."

Grinning, she stepped closer to him. "Nathan—"

"No, Lina, I need to tell y—"

"Hold on, I'm not finished yet." She held up her hand. "I know I'm going to probably talk really fast. Nerves, you know? But I want to just spill it all out and get it on the table before I chicken out or before you think I'm too crazy."

"I don't think you're crazy." He chuckled as she placed a restraining hand on his arm for him to be quiet.

"On my tenth date, I liked the guy. He was nice, kind, fun to be around. We had a great time." She squeezed closer to him as another couple nudged behind her at the bar. He smelled her perfume and liked that she reached for his hand when she stepped closer. "After the date, we went for a walk in the park and this drugged out thug came out of nowhere. He wanted money. He had a box cutter blade drawn and was pretty erratic as he swiped it through the air."

Nathan didn't like the direction her story was headed. "Did he hurt you?"

"No. Thankfully. But the point of me telling you all this is that my date just stood there. Actually, I take that back, he didn't stand there, he backed away. He left me there to fend for myself. He didn't even try to protect me or help me, he just faded into the background. I... well, I tased the guy. The thug, not my date," she amended. "And I ran." Her hands were moving wildly in the confined space between them as she conveyed the night's events and when she paused for a breath, Nathan reclasped her hands in his.

"I'm glad you're safe. You were smart. Most people wouldn't have a t—"

"I know. Luke already told me as much. But it just reminded me of our time on the subway when those teens were being obnoxious and punched you in the face."

"Okay..." He still didn't quite like that it sounded like he was beaten up by teenagers.

"When we were on the subway and all of that nonsense started happening, you tucked me into your side. Do you remember?"

"Yes."

"And you pulled me tighter and tighter until you had to branch away to deter their punches towards you. You protected me. You barely knew me, and you still protected me."

"If I recall, you protected me by waving your shoe at them," he added.

She grinned. "But not until you'd stood your ground for me. Nathan, it's all I could think about after my date with number ten. I wanted a man who'd protect me, stand with me, attempt to at least shield me if need be. Yes, I handled myself, but man, it sure would have been nice to have some support and strength backing me up. You did all of those things. And it made me wish to see you again. I didn't respond to your message that night because I was so drained from the experience, I didn't feel like I was thinking straight. I longed to see you and talk with you about it, but at the same time, that confused me."

"I understand that. I thought about you a lot while I was gone. Kicking myself for having to leave after having such a great time with you. I was so frustrated that last night."

"Well, you did have a split lip."

"Not because of that, though it didn't help," he laughed. "My job is just frustrating at times. I hated that I had to leave so abruptly, but that's how it is sometimes. In fact, my boss wanted me to turn around and leave again this week."

Lina's face sobered. "And are you?"

"No. I need a break. Mentally." He saw her face flood with relief, and he stood, stepping closer to her. "And, because I wanted to see you and pick up where we left off."

"Getting beat up by teenagers?"

He feigned being wounded and then stepped even closer to her. "Not exactly. Remember before I left, I'd planned to kiss you?"

"Did you?" Lina's eyes sparkled as she looked up at him, her hand gently resting against his chest.

"You shut me down though."

She guffawed at that and he grinned. "I'd like you to know, Evangelina Harper, that I no longer have a split lip and I plan on kissing you tonight." Or so he thought, but his plan was swiped out from under him when she pressed her lips to his in a nervous, enthusiastic kiss that struck his heart and sent an electric current of excitement straight through him. He cupped her face in his hands as she began to pull away. "And I was nervous you wouldn't want me to kiss you." He lightly brushed his lips over hers once more before tugging her away from the bar. "What do you say to a giant slice of chocolate cake and some beef jerky in the park instead?"

"You know, Number Eleven, I think that sounds like a fantastic plan." Lina grinned as he laughed.

"I think you mean, Number Seven."

"Hm... I guess you're right. I guess you're right."

Epilogue

Three Months Later

"Asa, I'll be there in five minutes. Just keep Mr. Rigsby comfortable in the conference room. His manuscript is on my desk and ready to go. Once I get there, I'll go over his edits with him." Lina paused to look up at the crosswalk light and then flashed a quick glance over to Trevor's coffee shop. She'd make the trip to fuel herself for what looked to be a long morning. Mr. Rigsby, the author of her current manuscript assignment, had arrived over an hour early for his appointment with her. He could wait an extra ten minutes until she even arrived to work. "I'm getting you a coffee," she told Asa. "What's your poison?" She recited his order in her mind two times so as not to forget, though she knew Asa would be happy with any caffeinated beverage she brought him. "Okay, see you in a few minutes." She hung up and stepped inside the warm and friendly atmosphere of Trevor's. Smiling, she spotted Nathan in line ahead of her. She walked up and stood next to him. "What will it be, Seven?"

He uncrossed his arms and wrapped one around her shoulders and tugged her to him. "Good morning to you too, my sweet Evangelina." He roamed his eyes over her face, and she stood on her tip toes to give him a kiss. "You smell good." He directed his nose to the crook of her neck, and she laughed.

"Stop that."

He reluctantly pulled away as she waved at Trevor.

"And how has your morning started out?" Nathan asked.

"Oh, Mr. Rigsby is already at the office, Asa is freaking out, and me, well, I wanted to see my boyfriend before heading into the office."

"Sounds like your morning is going better than Asa's." Nathan smirked as they stepped forward together.

"That's why I'm going to treat him to a drink."

"On me," Nathan added.

Trevor greeted them and quickly created their different drinks, along with Asa's, and sent them on their way, each with a free pastry. "He spoils us." Lina took a hearty bite of her muffin as she grabbed extra napkins. "So, what does your day look like today? Fighting bad guys? Bringing down a dark and mysterious hacker?"

Nathan laughed. "Nothing so glamorous. I'm office duty today with Luke. We have some paperwork to wrap up on the Gibson case."

"And you didn't believe Luke." She shook her head in disappointment.

Nathan held up a finger. "Not that I didn't believe Gibson was dirty, we just needed the proof."

"And now you have it."

"Yes. Luke found the proof we needed."

"And all is well?"

"Will be once we arrest everyone involved, which is underway. But I don't have to help with that area. My work is strictly on the cyber side this go around."

"I'm glad." Lina finished off her muffin and took a long sip of her coffee. "I better get. My day is starting earlier than planned."

Nathan's green gaze washed over her outfit, her face, and then her lips, causing her stomach to flutter. "Will I be seeing you at lunch?"

"Probably not." Lina frowned. "I will probably be treating Mr. Rigsby to lunch, courtesy of Armm and Goode."

"Ah. Well, I guess it's a long day for me then."

"Why is that?"

"Because I won't get to see you until quitting time."

"You'll wait for me at the crosswalk?" she asked, knowing he would. That'd been their routine since they officially started dating. They'd meet for coffee in the morning, walk to work together, split their separate ways, and at the end of the day, he was always waiting for her on the other side of the crosswalk. His charming smile, handsome face, and strong presence always welcoming after a long day. Andy had yet to give up her annoying habit of taking credit for their romance, but Lina was growing less bothered by that nuisance. She had Nathan now, and that was all that mattered. Lucky number seven, she mused. A blind date she'd never forget, and a man she'd always love.

He kissed her tenderly and slowly before answering, "I'll be there."

All titles in The Lighthearted Collection Available in Paperback, Ebook, and Audiobook

Chicago's Best
https://www.amazon.com/dp/B06XH7Y3MF

Montgomery House
https://www.amazon.com/dp/B073T1SVCN

Beautiful Fury
https://www.amazon.com/dp/B07B527N57

McCarthy Road
https://www.amazon.com/dp/B08NF5HYJG

The Complete Siblings O'Rifcan Series Available in Paperback, Ebook, and Audiobook

Claron
https://www.amazon.com/dp/B07FYR44KX

Riley
https://www.amazon.com/dp/B07G2RBD8D

Layla
https://www.amazon.com/dp/B07HJRL67M

Chloe
https://www.amazon.com/dp/B07KB3HG6B

Murphy
https://www.amazon.com/dp/B07N4FCY8V

The Brothers of Hastings Ranch Series Available in Paperback, Ebook, and Audiobook

Graham
https://www.amazon.com/dp/B08777YG9R

Calvin
https://www.amazon.com/dp/B087N9DL7T

Philip
https://www.amazon.com/dp/B08B2QZZSB

Lawrence
https://www.amazon.com/dp/B08JWT8Y8N

Hayes
https://www.amazon.com/dp/B08QDJJ9PW

**Check out the Epic Fantasy Adventure
Available in Paperback, Ebook, and
Audiobook**

U^{THE}NFADING LANDS

The Unfading Lands

https://www.amazon.com/dp/B00VKWKPES

Darkness Divided, Part Two in The Unfading Lands Series

https://www.amazon.com/dp/B015QFTAXG

Redemption Rising, Part Three in The Unfading Lands Series

https://www.amazon.com/dp/B01G5NYSEO

Subscribe to Katharine's Newsletter for news on upcoming releases and events!
https://www.katharinehamilton.com/subscribe.html

Find out more about Katharine and her works at:
www.katharinehamilton.com

Social Media is a great way to connect with Katharine. Check her out on the following:

Facebook: Katharine E. Hamilton
https://www.facebook.com/Katharine-E-Hamilton-282475125097433/

Twitter: @AuthorKatharine
Instagram: @AuthorKatharine

Contact Katharine:
khamiltonauthor@gmail.com

ABOUT THE AUTHOR

Katharine E. Hamilton began writing in 2008 and published her first children's book, The Adventurous Life of Laura Bell in 2009. She would go on to write and illustrate two more children's books, Susie At Your Service and Sissy and Kat between 2010-2013.

Though writing for children was fun, Katharine moved into Adult Fiction in 2015 with her release of The Unfading Lands, a clean, epic fantasy that landed in Amazon's Hot 100 New Releases on its fourth day of publication, reached #72 in the Top 100 in Epic Fantasy, and hit the Top 10,000 Best Sellers on all of Amazon in its first week. It has been listed as a Top 100 Indie Read for 2015 and a nominee for a Best Indie Book Award for 2016. The series did not stop there. Darkness Divided: Part Two of The Unfading Land Series, released in October of 2015 and claimed a spot in the Top 100 of its genre. Redemption Rising: Part Three of The Unfading Lands Series released in April 2016 and claimed a nomination for the Summer Indie Book Awards.

Though comfortable in the fantasy genre, Katharine decided to venture towards romance in 2017 and released the first novel in a collection of sweet, clean and wholesome romances: The Lighthearted Collection. Chicago's Best reached best seller status in its first week of publication and rested comfortably in the Top 100 for Amazon for three steady weeks, claimed a Reader's Choice Award, a TopShelf Indie Book Award, and ended up a finalist in the American Book Festival's

Best Book Awards for 2017. <u>Montgomery House</u>, the second in the collection, released in August of 2017 and rested comfortably alongside its predecessor, claiming a Reader's Choice Award, and becoming Katharine's best-selling novel up to that point. Both were released in audiobook format in late 2017 and early 2018. <u>Beautiful Fury</u> is the third novel released in the collection and has claimed a Reader's Choice Award and a gold medal in the Authorsdb Best Cover competition. It has also been released in audiobook format with narrator Chelsea Carpenter lending her talents to bring it to life. Katharine and Chelsea have partnered on an ongoing project for creating audiobook marketing methods for fellow authors and narrators, all of which will eventually be published as a resource tool for others.

In August of 2018, Katharine brought to life a new clean contemporary romance series of a loving family based in Ireland. The Siblings O'Rifcan Series kicked off in August with <u>Claron</u>. <u>Claron</u> climbed to the Top 1000 of the entire Amazon store and has reached the Top 100 of the Clean and Wholesome genre a total of 11 times. He is Katharine's bestselling book thus far and lends to the success of the following books in the series: <u>Riley</u>, <u>Layla</u>, <u>Chloe</u>, and <u>Murphy,</u> each book earning their place in the Top 100 of their genre and Hot 100 New Releases. <u>Claron</u> was featured in Amazon's Prime Reading program March – June 2019. The series is also available in audiobook format with the voice talents of Alex Black.

A Love For All Seasons, a Sweet Contemporary Romance Series launched in July of 2019 with

Summer's Catch, followed by Autumn's Fall in October. Winter's Call and Spring's Hope scheduled for 2021 release dates. The series follows a wonderful group of friends from Friday Harbor, Washington, and has been Katharine's newest and latest project.

Her series The Brothers of Hastings Ranch has topped the charts since its debut of Graham in April of 2019 and will contain a total of seven books.

Katharine has contributed to charitable Indie Anthologies as well as helped other aspiring writers journey their way through the publication process. She manages an online training course that walks fellow self-publishing and independently publishing writers through the publishing process as well as how to market their books.

She is a member of Women Fiction Writers of America, Texas Authors, IASD, and the American Christian Fiction Writers. She loves everything to do with writing and loves that she is able to continue sharing heartwarming stories to a wide array of readers.

Katharine graduated from Texas A&M University with a bachelor's degree in History. She lives on a ranch in south Texas with her husband Brad, son Everett, another son on the way, West, and their two dogs, Tulip and Paws.